Dreams of Dreams

and

The Last Three Days of Fernando Pessoa

Dreams of Dreams

and

The Last Three Days
of Fernando Pessoa

by Antonio Tabucchi

Translated from the Italian by Nancy J. Peters

City Lights
San Francisco

Sogni di sogni @ 1992 by Selerio Editore, Palermo
Gli ultimi tre giorni di Fernando Pessoa @ 1994 by Editions du Seuil.
Translation copyright © 1999 by Nancy J. Peters
All Rights Reserved
10 9 8 7 6 5 4 3 2 1

Cover design: RexRay
Book design: Elaine Katzenberger
Typography: Harvest Graphics

Library of Congress Cataloging-in-Publication Data

Tabucchi, Antonio, 1943
    [Sogni di sogni. English]
    Dreams of dreams: and, The last three days of Fernando Pessoa /
by Antonio Tabucchi ; translated from the Italian by Nancy J. Peters.
      p.   cm.
    ISBN 0-87286-368-9
    1. Ovid, 43 B.C.-17 or 18 A.D.—Fiction.   2. Pessoa, Fernando,
1888-1935—Fiction.   I. Title: Dreams of dreams; and, The last
three days of Fernando Pessoa.   II. Peters, Nancy J. (Nancy Joyce)
III. Tabucchi, Antonio, 1943- Gli ultimi tre giorni di Fernando
Pessoa. English.   IV. Title: Last three days of Fernando Pessoa.
V. Title.
PQ4880.A24 S6413 2000
853'.914—dc21

                                          99-087459

CITY LIGHTS BOOKS are edited by Lawrence Ferlinghetti and
Nancy J. Peters and published at the City Lights Bookstore,
261 Columbus Avenue, San Francisco CA 94133

I wish to thank James Brook, Lawrence Ferlinghetti, Giampiero Benvenuti, and David H. Davis for helpful suggestions; Amelia Antonucci, Director of the Istituto Italiano di Cultura in San Francisco for her support of Italian and American literary exchanges; Greti Croft, friend and teacher; and most especially Stefánia Benini for her invaluable close reading of the translation.

—N.J.P.

CONTENTS

$\sim$

Dreams of Dreams

to my daughter Teresa,
who gave me
the notebook
in which this book was born

Under the almond tree of your woman,
when the first August moon rises behind the house,
you'll be able to dream,
if the gods are smiling, the dreams of another.

—*Ancient Chinese song*

I have often been seized by the desire to know the dreams of artists I have loved. Unfortunately, those who speak in this book have not left us the nocturnal trajectories of their minds. The temptation to remedy this in some way is great, to call on literature to provide what has been lost. Yet I am aware that these vicarious narrations — which one nostalgic for unknown dreams has tried to imagine — are only poor suppositions, pale illusions, implausible projections. May they be read as such, and may the souls of my characters, now dreaming on the Other Side, be indulgent with their poor descendent.

—A.T.

DREAM OF DAEDALUS,
ARCHITECT AND AVIATOR

One night, thousands of years ago, at a time impossible to calculate exactly, Daedalus, architect and aviator, had a dream.

He dreamed that he was deep inside an immense palace and he was going through a corridor. The corridor opened into another corridor and Daedalus, tired and confused, walked along it, leaning on the walls. When he had come to the end, the corridor opened into a small octagonal room, from which eight corridors branched out. Daedalus began to feel short of breath and a need for fresh air. He entered one corridor, but it ended against a wall. He went into another, but it too ended against a wall. Seven times Daedalus made an attempt until, on the eighth attempt, he entered a very long corridor that, after a series of curves and corners, led out into another corridor. Daedalus then sat down on a marble step and began to reflect. On the corridor walls were flaming torches that illuminated frescoes blue with birds and flowers.

I'm the only one who could know how to get out of here, Daedalus said to himself, and I don't remember. He took off his sandals and began to walk barefoot on the green marble floor.

To console himself, he began to sing an ancient dirge he

had learned from an old servant who had rocked his infant cradle. The arcades of the long corridor carried his voice back to him ten times over.

I'm the only one who could know how to get out of here, said Daedalus, and I don't remember.

At that moment, he came out into a wide, circular room frescoed with absurd landscapes. He remembered that room but he couldn't remember why he remembered it. There were seats covered with luxurious fabrics and, in the middle of the room, a large bed. On the edge of the bed was seated a slender man with youthful and lively features. And that man had the head of a bull. He was holding his head between his hands and sobbing. Daedalus approached him and put his hand on his shoulder. Why are you crying? he asked. The man lifted his head from his hands and stared at him with his animal gaze. I'm crying because I'm in love with the moon, he said. I saw her only once, when I was a child at the window, but I can't reach her because I'm imprisoned in this palace. I would be happy just to stretch out in a meadow during the night and let myself be kissed by her rays, but I'm imprisoned in this palace, and since childhood I've been imprisoned in this palace. And he began to cry again.

And then Daedalus felt a great longing, and his heart pounded in his chest. I will help you get out of here, he said.

The man-beast raised his head again and stared at him with his bovine eyes. In this room there are two doors, he said, and there are two guardians to guard each door. One door leads to freedom, and one door leads to death. One of the guardians tells only the truth, and the other tells only lies. But I don't know which guardian tells the truth or which one lies, or which is the door to freedom and which the one to death.

Follow me, said Daedalus. Come with me.

He approached one of the guardians and asked him: Which is the door that, according to your colleague, leads to freedom? And then he took the other door. Indeed, if he had consulted the lying guardian, the latter, altering the indications of his colleague, would have pointed to the door of doom; if, instead, he had consulted the truthful guardian, the latter would give him unchanged the false indication of his colleague, who would have pointed to the door of death.

They passed through that other door and again traveled along a lengthy corridor. The corridor rose up and opened out into a hanging garden, overlooking the lights of an unknown city.

Now Daedalus remembered, and he was glad to remember. Under the bushes were hidden feathers and wax. He had done this himself in order to flee from that palace. From those feathers and that wax he ably constructed a pair of wings and affixed them to the back of the man-beast. Then he led him to the railing of the hanging garden and spoke to him.

The night is long, he said. The moon shows her face and waits for you. Now you can fly to her.

The man-beast turned and gazed at him with his soft animal eyes. Thank you, he said.

Go, said Daedalus, and gave him a push. He watched the man-beast who moved off into the night with wide strokes and flew toward the moon. And he flew and he flew.

DREAM OF PUBLIUS OVIDIUS NASO, POET AND COURTIER

In Tomi, on the Black Sea, on the 16th of January after Christ's birth, on a night of ice and storm, Publius Ovidius Naso, poet and courtier, dreamed that he had become a poet beloved by the emperor. And as such, by a miracle of the gods, he was transformed into a great butterfly.

He was an enormous butterfly, as big as a man, with majestic yellow and blue wings. And his eyes, the immense spherical eyes of a butterfly, embraced the whole horizon.

They had hoisted him up into a golden chariot, prepared expressly for him, and three pairs of white horses were bringing him to Rome. He tried to stand up, but his thin legs couldn't bear the weight of his wings, so every now and then he was obliged to recline on cushions, his feet kicking in the air. On his legs he wore Oriental bracelets and jewelry that he displayed with pride to the applauding crowd.

When they arrived at the gates of Rome, Ovid got up from the cushions and with great effort, struggling on swaying legs, encircled his head with a crown of laurel.

The crowd became ecstatic and many people prostrated themselves because they believed he was an Asian divinity.

Now Ovid wanted to alert them that he was Ovid, and he began to speak. But from his mouth issued a strange hiss, a shrill, unbearable whistle that made the people in the crowd cover their ears with their hands.

Don't you hear my song, cried Ovid, this is the song of the poet Ovid, the one who taught the art of love, who told of courtiers and rogues, of miracles and metamorphoses!

But his voice was an indistinct whistle, and the crowd scattered before the horses. Finally they arrived at the imperial palace and Ovid clumsily got to his feet, went up the stairway that took him to Caesar.

Seated on his throne, the emperor awaited him, and he was drinking a tankard of wine. Let us hear something you have composed for me, said Caesar.

Ovid had written a small poem of nimble verses, artful and witty, that would delight Caesar. But how to recite them, he wondered, if his voice was only the hiss of an insect. And so he decided to communicate his verses to Caesar with gestures and gently began to move his majestic colored wings in a marvelous and exotic ballet. The palace curtains shook, an annoying wind swept through the rooms, and Caesar flung his tankard to the floor in irritation. Caesar was a surly man who loved frugality and virility. He couldn't stand it that this indecent insect would perform that effeminate ballet in front of him. He clapped his hands and the praetorian guards rushed forward.

Soldiers, said Caesar, cut off his wings! The guards unsheathed their swords and deftly lopped off Ovid's wings, as if he were a tree. The wings fell to the ground like soft feathers and Ovid understood at that moment that his life was ending. Moved by a power he felt to be his destiny, he made an about-face and, swaying on his atrocious insect legs, returned to the palace terrace. Below was a ferocious crowd that clamored for its spoils, an avid crowd waiting for him with furious hands.

And then, hopping clumsily, Ovid descended the palace stairs.

DREAM OF LUCIUS APULEIUS,
WRITER AND MAGICIAN

On an October night in 165 AD, in the city of Carthage, Lucius Apuleius, writer and magician, had a dream. He dreamed that he was in a small Numidian town. It was evening in a torrid African summer. He was walking near the main gates of the city when he was attracted by laughter and commotion. He went through the gate and saw near the red clay walls a group of acrobats putting on a show. One semi-naked acrobat, his body painted with white lead, was balancing precariously on a rope, pretending to be on the point of falling. The crowd was laughing and apprehensive, and dogs were barking. Then the acrobat lost his balance, but remained hanging there, clinging with one hand to the rope. The crowd broke into a cry of terror and then applauded happily. The acrobats turned a winch that held the rope taut, and the acrobat let himself down to the ground, making funny faces. A piper came forward into the circle of packed-down earth lit by glints of firelight and began to play Oriental music. And then from a wagon stepped a full-breasted woman, covered with veils, who held a whip in her hand. The woman advanced, whipping the air; and she wound the whip around her body.

She was a woman with dark-brown hair and eyes ringed with dark circles, and, because she was sweating, her makeup ran down her face.

Apuleius would have liked to leave, but a mysterious force obliged him to stay, to keep his eyes fixed on the woman. The drums began to play, at first slowly and then in a frenzy, and at that point, from under the big tent where the animals were kept, came four majestic white horses and one poor, tired ass. The dancer cracked the whip and the horses reared, prancing out at carousel speed. The ass lay down on one side, near the monkey cages, and slowly began to swish flies with its tail. The dancer cracked the whip again, and the horses stopped and knelt, emitting long neighs. Then the woman, with surprising agility given her corpulence, took a leap and, keeping one foot on one horse and one foot on another, began to ride two animals, standing up with her legs spread open above their backs. And as they galloped, she obscenely shook the handle of the whip in front of her belly while the crowd murmured with delight. Then the drums stopped beating and the tired ass, as if it were obeying an invisible command, turned over on its back with its hooves in the air, and it exhibited to the public its erect phallus. The woman, turning around, shouted that for the continuation of the performance only those could remain who had paid hard cash, and two acrobats dressed as guards, equipped with whips, chased away the children and beggars.

Apuleius was alone, in the circle of the few. He took two silver coins out of his bag, paid, then began to watch the performance. The woman grasped the ass's phallus and, lustily fondling it against her belly, began to dance a languid dance, removing the veils to display her charms. Apuleius approached and raised a hand, and then the ass opened its mouth, but instead of braying it uttered human words.

I am Lucius, he said. Don't you recognize me?

Which Lucius? asked Apuleius.

Your Lucius, said the ass, the one from your adventures, your friend Lucius.

Apuleius looked around, convinced that the voice came from somewhere nearby, but the door in the wall was already closed, the sentinels were sleeping, and behind him breathed the silence of the deep African night.

This witch put a curse on me, said the ass. She imprisoned me in this semblance. Only you can free me, you who are a writer and magician.

Apuleius leapt toward the fire and seized a blazing firebrand, traced signs in the air, pronounced the words he knew should be pronounced. The woman screamed, her mouth made a grimace of disgust and her face grew wrinkled, assuming the appearance of an old woman. Then, as if by magic, the woman dissolved into thin air, and with her disappeared the acrobats, the walled enclosure, the African night. Suddenly it was day: it was a splendid bright day in Rome. Apuleius walked along the Forum and his friend Lucius walked by his side. Strolling along, they chatted, while they looked at the most beautiful slaves that wandered through the market. At a certain point, Apuleius stopped and, seizing Lucius by his toga, looked him in the eye and said to him: last night I had a dream.

DREAM OF CECCO ANGIOLIERI,
POET AND BLASPHEMER

One night in January 1309, while lying on a straw mattress in the Sienna leper hospital, wrapped in nauseating bandages, Cecco Angiolieri, poet and blasphemer, had a dream. He dreamed it was a torrid summer day and that he was passing in front of the cathedral. Knowing the place was cool he planned to go inside to escape the midsummer heat, but instead of genuflecting and dipping his fingers in holy water, he crossed his fingers in a magical sign of protection because he feared the place would bring him bad luck.

In the first chapel to the right there was a painter who was painting a Madonna. The painter was a blond youth and, with the palette on his arm, he was seated on a stool in an attitude of repose. The holy picture was almost finished: it was a Virgin with oblique eyes and an imperceptible smile, holding on her knees the baby Jesus, who lay in the folds of her garments. The painter greeted him courteously. Cecco Angiolieri responded with an outburst of laughter. Then he began to look at the painting and he felt a great uneasiness. The expression of that haughty woman annoyed him, she grandly watched the world as if she greatly disdained earthly things. He couldn't resist its power: he approached the painting and, raising his right arm, gave it an obscene gesture. The young painter leapt to his feet and tried to stop him, but Cecco Angiolieri, like a man possessed, twisted around and made an obscene gesture with his left arm too. Then the virgin moved her eyes as if they were human eyes and struck him with her gaze. Cecco Angiolieri felt a strange shiver run through his whole body, he began to become numb and grow smaller. He saw that his limbs were becoming covered with black fur, he grew aware that a long tail sprouted between his legs and he tried to yell, but instead of a yell coming out of his mouth there came a terrifying meow, and, small and furious at the painter's feet, he realized that he had become a cat. He made one leap ahead and another backward, as if crazed in the monstrous prison of that new body. He gritted his furious teeth and left the church meowing savagely. Meanwhile, night was falling on the piazza. At first Cecco Angiolieri crept along the walls and then he looked around to see if anyone was watching him. But the square was almost deserted. At the corner near a tavern stood a group of malicious-looking boys who had carried tankards outside, and they were drinking. Cecco Angiolieri intended to pass along the front of the tavern, because he was hungry, and perhaps he could find a crust of cheese. He crept along the tavern wall and passed in front of the door, which was lit by two torches on the doorjambs. Just then, one of the hoodlums called him, making the typical sound of the lips used to call cats and showed him some prosciutto rind. Cecco Angiolieri hurried to his feet and seized the rind in his mouth, but at that very moment the boys grabbed him and, holding him tight, carried him into the tavern. Cecco Angiolieri tried to bite and scratch, but the malicious boys held him fast, squeezing his mouth closed and immobilizing his paws, so that nothing could be done. When they were inside, the boys took the oil container that fed the torch and spread the oil thoroughly through his fur. Then they set him on fire with the torch and set him free.

Transformed into a ball of fire, Cecco Angiolieri dashed outside, meowing horribly; he threw himself against the walls of houses, he rolled on the ground but the fire would not go out. Like an arrow, he began to crisscross the dark, narrow streets of Sienna, lighting them up as he went. He didn't know where to go, he let instinct carry him along. He turned two corners, he ran through three streets, he crossed a small piazza, went up a stairway and arrived in front of a palace. His father lived there. Cecco Angiolieri ascended the grand staircase, went past the terrified servants, entered the dining room, where his father was eating dinner, and howled: Father, I've become a fire, please, save me! And at that moment Cecco Angiolieri woke up. The physicians removed his bandages and, covered with the terrible sores of St. Anthony's fire, his body burned like flame.

DREAM OF FRANÇOIS VILLON, POET AND MALEFACTOR

Christmas dawn, 1451, while submerged in the last stages of sleep, François Villon, poet and malefactor, had a dream. He dreamed it was a night of the full moon and that he was crossing a desolate moor. He stopped to eat a piece of bread that he pulled out of his knapsack, and he sat down on a rock. He looked at the sky and felt a great anguish. Then he proceeded on his way and arrived at an inn. The house was dark and silent, perhaps everyone was asleep. François Villon knocked insistently at the door, and the innkeeper's wife opened it for him.

What are you looking for at this hour, wayfarer? asked the innkeeper's wife, illuminating Villon's face with the lantern.

I'm looking for my brother, answered François Villon. I saw him last in these parts and I want to find him.

He entered the dark inn, lit only by a dim fire, and he sat down at a table.

I want mutton and wine, he ordered, and began to wait. The innkeeper's wife brought him a plate of leftover potatoes and a pitcher of cider. It's what we've got this evening, she said. Cheer up, wayfarer, because the police roam these parts and they've finished off all our food.

25

While Villon was eating, an old man came in, his face covered by rags. He was a leper, and he was leaning on a walking stick. François Villon looked at him and said nothing. The leper sat down across the room near the fire, and he said: They told me you're looking for your brother.

Villon's hand ran quickly to his dagger, but the leper stopped him with a gesture. I'm not on the side of the police, he said. I'm on the criminals' side and I can lead you to your brother. Leaning on his stick, he went toward the door and Villon followed him. They went out into the winter cold. It was a clear night and the snow on the fields was icy. Around them was a barren moor, edged by the black profile of hills covered with woods. The leper took a path and wearily headed for the hills. Villon followed him; meanwhile, he kept his hand on his dagger for safety.

When the road began to ascend, the leper stopped and sat down on a rock. He took an ocarina from his knapsack and began to play a nostalgic melody. Every once in a while he interrupted himself and sang a few stanzas from a bloodthirsty ballad that told of rapes and evil-doers, holdups and gendarmes. Villon listened to him and shuddered because he knew the ballad was about him. And then he felt a sort of fear, which assailed him in the pit of his stomach. But fear of what? He didn't know, because he wasn't afraid of the gendarmes, nor did he fear the dark or the leper. He sensed that his fear was a kind of remorse, a kind of subtle sorrow.

Then the leper got up, and Villon followed him into the woods. When they came to the first tree, Villon saw that a hanged man was swinging from the branches. His tongue was hanging out, and the moonlight shone dimly on the corpse. He was an unknown man, and Villon went on ahead. And from the next tree hung another man, but he didn't know this one, either. Villon looked around and saw that the woods were full of corpses dangling from the trees. He looked at them, one by one, serenely, as he wandered among the feet that were swaying in the breeze, until he found his brother. He cut him down, severing the rope with the dagger, and he laid him on the grass. The corpse was rigid from death and cold. François Villon kissed his brow. And at that moment, his brother's corpse spoke. Life here is full of white butterflies that are waiting for you, my brother, said the corpse, and they are all larvae.

Confused, François Villon raised his head. His companion had disappeared and, from the woods, like a great funeral chorus softly intoned, swelled the ballad the leper sang.

DREAM OF FRANÇOIS RABELAIS, WRITER AND FORMER FRIAR

One night in February 1532, at the hospital in Lyons, while he was sleeping in his small, austere doctor's room, after seven days of fasting in observance of the rules of conventual life that he continued to follow even after he had left the order, François Rabelais, writer and former friar, had a dream. He dreamed that he was under the pergola of an inn in Périgord, and that it was the month of September. There was a long narrow table, set with a white tablecloth and covered with carafes of wine, and he was seated at the head of the table. The opposite end of the table was set for another person, but he didn't know for whom, he only knew that he had to wait. While he was waiting, the innkeeper brought him a plate of marinated olives and a tankard of fresh cider, and he began to nibble, sipping that exquisite cider of a beautiful amber color. At a certain point he heard a shuffle of clogs and saw a cloud of dust approaching on the main road. It was a coach of regal appearance, with a coachman dressed in red and two footmen on the footboards. The coach stopped on the tavern lawn, the two footmen sounded two blasts on trumpets and then stepped down smartly, spreading out a red carpet in front of the coach door. They stood at attention and cried: His Majesty Sir Pantagruel, king of food and wine! François Rabelais stood up because he understood that his dining companion had arrived, that he was at that very moment advancing majestically on the red carpet the footmen had unfurled at his feet. He was a man of gigantic stature who held his belly in his hands as he walked, an enormous belly, fat as a wineskin, that swung from side to side. He had a thick black beard that framed his face, and on his head he wore a big hat with a wide brim. His majesty Sir Pantagruel opened his mouth in a huge smile, he rolled up the sleeves of his regal garb and sat down at the other end of the table. The innkeeper arrived, preceding a steaming soup tureen carried by two pages, and began to serve. A soup of barley, wheat, and beans, he announced as he served, a little something to whet the appetite. His majesty Sir Pantagruel tied a napkin as big as a sheet around his neck and signaled to François Rabelais that he could begin. It was a grain soup in which swam laurel leaves and garlic cloves, a truly delicate appetizer. François Rabelais ate a plate of it with gusto, while his majesty Sir Pantagruel, after politely asking his permission, approached the tureen and began to drink the soup right down. Meanwhile, the valets kept coming with other food, while the attentive innkeeper refilled the plates. This time it was stuffed goose. They served François Rabelais two geese, and nineteen to Sir Pantagruel. Innkeeper, said his majesty the guest, you must teach me how these geese are cooked. I want to tell my cook. The innkeeper smoothed his imposing mustache, cleared his throat and said: first you take a fine choucroute and put it to the boil for four or five minutes. Then you melt the goose fat and sauté the cabbage, lard, juniper berries, cloves, salt and pepper, sliced onion, and then cook it for three hours. Then you add prosciutto, finely chopped goose liver, and you bind the mixture with bread crumbs. The geese are filled with this stuffing and put into the oven for about forty minutes. You have to remember, when it's half-cooked, to collect the sizzling fat and pour it over the stuffing, and the dish is ready. Hearing this description made François Rabelais hungry again, and his dinner companion too, at least by the look of him, because he was licking his mustache with his gigantic tongue, finally asking, and now, innkeeper, what do you suggest? The innkeeper clapped his hands and servants arrived bearing steaming vessels.

Capons in plum grappa and guinea hens with Roquefort, said the innkeeper with satisfaction, and he began to serve. François Rabelais began to eat a capon and a guinea hen with gusto, while his majesty Sir Pantagruel devoured a dozen of them. I don't know why, said Sir Pantagruel, but I think that these capons would go well with a sauce of brains, what do you say, my dear dining companion? François Rabelais nodded and the innkeeper, as if he expected nothing else, clapped his hands. The servants brought two vessels overflowing with brain sauce. His majesty Sir Pantagruel spread one vesselful on a yard-long loaf of bread, and between one mouthful of capon and the next, with so many bitty bites, he consumed it all in two minutes. When they had finished, the innkeeper asked permission to clear away the dirty plates and he asked: What would you say, gentlemen, to a little wild boar cacciatora, or would you prefer filet of stuffed and sautéed hare? For the sake of fairness, François Rabelais proposed that he bring both. And his majesty Sir Pantagruel yawned to indicate that he was still hungry. The innkeeper clapped his hands and the servants came in with the new dishes. While eating, he managed to mutter how supremely delicious was that boar cacciatora! A subtly-sweet-and sour cacciatora with green olives and a smidgen of peppers to bring out the wild flavor. And the sautéed and stuffed filets of rabbit, responded his majesty Sir Pantagruel, couldn't they perhaps be called divine?

The innkeeper watched them eat with a blissful air. It was September and the sun etched bright spots in the shade of the pergola. His majesty Sir Pantagruel had little tiny eyes and he lowered his lids now and then as if he were falling asleep. Then he clapped his belly with the palm of his hand, politely asked permission, and discharged a formidable belch, a roar that seemed a thunderclap resounding through the countryside. François Rabelais woke to the roar of thunder and saw that it was a stormy night. Fumbling to turn on the light, he grabbed from the night table a piece of dry bread, which he allowed himself every night to break his fast.

DREAM OF MICHELANGELO MERISI, CALLED CARAVAGGIO, PAINTER AND IRASCIBLE MAN

On the night of January 1, 1599, while he was in bed with a prostitute, Michelangelo Merisi, called Caravaggio, painter and irascible man, dreamed that God visited him. God was visiting him through Christ, and He was pointing His finger at him. Michelangelo was in a tavern and he was gambling for money. His companions were sharpers, and some of them were drunk. And he, he was not Michelangelo Merisi, the celebrated painter, but just an ordinary customer, a ruffian. When God visited him he was cursing the name of Christ, and he was laughing. You, the finger of Christ said wordlessly. Me? asked the astonished Michelangelo Merisi. I'm not a saint by vocation, I'm just a sinner. I can't be chosen.

But Christ's expression was inflexible, no escape. And His extended hand left no room for doubt.

Michelangelo Merisi lowered his head and looked at the money on the table. I've raped, he said, I've killed. I'm a man with blood on his hands. The waiter at the tavern came carrying beans and wine. Michelangelo Merisi began to eat and drink.

Everyone near him was immobilized, he alone was moving

his hands and his mouth like a ghost. Even Christ was motionless and holding out his hand motionless, with His finger pointed. Michelangelo Merisi got up and followed Him. They went out into a filthy alley, and Michelangelo Merisi began to urinate in a corner all the wine he had drunk that evening.

God, why do You seek me? Michelangelo Merisi asked Christ. The Son of Man looked at him without answering. They walked through the alley and entered a piazza. The piazza was deserted.

I'm sad, said Michelangelo Merisi. Christ looked at him and didn't answer. He sat down on a stone bench and took off His sandals. He massaged His feet and said, I'm tired. I've come on foot from Palestine to look for you.

Michelangelo Merisi was vomiting as he leaned against the wall at the corner. But I'm a sinner, he cried, you shouldn't be looking for me!

Christ approached and touched his arm. I made you a painter, He said, and I want a painting from you. Afterward you can follow the road of your destiny.

Michelangelo Merisi wiped his mouth and asked: What painting?

The visit I paid you tonight in the tavern, except you'll be Matthew.

All right, said Michelangelo Merisi. I'll do it. And he turned over in bed, and at that moment the prostitute embraced him, snoring.

DREAM OF FRANCISCO GOYA Y LUCIENTES, PAINTER AND VISIONARY

The night of May 1, 1820, while visited by his intermittent madness, Francisco Goya y Lucientes, painter and visionary, had a dream.

He dreamed he was under a tree with the love of his youth. It was the austere countryside of Aragón and the sun was high. His sweetheart was on a swing, which he was pushing, his hands on her waist. His sweetheart held a lace umbrella and she laughed in short nervous bursts. Then she slipped down from the swing into the meadow, and he followed, tumbling over and over. They tumbled down the hillside until they came to a yellow wall. They faced the wall and saw soldiers illuminated by a lantern, who were shooting men. The lantern was incongruous in that sunny landscape, but it cast a strange pallor over the scene. The soldiers fired and the men fell into pools of their own blood. Then Francisco Goya y Lucientes pulled out the paintbrush that he kept at his belt and advanced, brandishing it menacingly. As if under a spell, the soldiers disappeared, terrified by the apparition. And in their place appeared a horrendous giant who was devouring a human leg. He had dirty hair and a livid face. Two streams of blood ran down to the corners of his mouth although he was laughing, and his eyes were veiled.

Who are you? asked Francisco Goya y Lucientes.

The giant wiped his mouth and said: I am the monster that rules human beings. History is my mother.

Francisco Goya y Lucientes took a step and brandished his paintbrush. The giant disappeared and in his place appeared an old woman. She was a toothless hag with parchment skin and yellow eyes.

Who are you? asked Francisco Goya y Lucientes.

I am disillusion, said the old woman, and I rule the world, because every human dream is a but a brief dream.

Francisco Goya y Lucientes took a step and brandished his paintbrush. The old woman disappeared and in her place appeared a dog. It was a small dog, buried in the sand, with only its head above ground.

Who are you? asked Francisco Goya y Lucientes.

The dog drew its head up and said: I am the beast of desperation and I mock your suffering.

Francisco Goya y Lucientes took a step and brandished his paintbrush. The dog disappeared and in its place appeared a man. He was a fat old man, with a flaccid and unhappy face.

Who are you? Francisco Goya y Lucientes asked him.

The man gave a weary smile and said: I am Francisco Goya y Lucientes, and against me you can do nothing.

At that moment, Francisco Goya y Lucientes woke up and found himself alone in his bed.

DREAM OF SAMUEL TAYLOR COLERIDGE,
POET AND OPIUM-EATER

One night in November 1801, in his London house, prey to opium delirium, Samuel Taylor Coleridge, poet and opium-eater, had a dream. He dreamed he was on a ship imprisoned in the ice. He was the captain, and his men, taking cover, were trying miserably to protect themselves from the cold, covering themselves with rags and torn blankets. They had emaciated faces, sickness in their eyes, which were lined with dark circles. A powerful albatross was sitting on the yardarm of the ship with its wings spread out, and it threw a menacing shadow on the bridge. Samuel Taylor Coleridge called his first mate and ordered him to bring him a gun, but he replied that there was no more gunpowder and handed him a crossbow. So Samuel Taylor Coleridge grabbed the crossbow and took aim. He thought that killing the albatross would enable him to feed his exhausted sailors, saving them from scurvy and death. He took aim and shot the bolt. The albatross, wounded in the neck by the arrow, fell onto the bridge and its blood sprayed the surrounding ice. And from the blood fallen on the ice was born a sea serpent who raised its jerking head and faced the bulwarks, hissing with its forked tongue. Samuel Taylor Coleridge seized the saber he wore at his waist and promptly cut off its head. And so from that severed head was born a thin woman dressed in black, with a pale face and haunted eyes. The woman held a pair of dice in her hand, sat down on the quarter-deck, and called to the captain. Now we must throw the dice, she said. If you win, your ship will go free. If I win, I'll take your sailors with me. The mate rushed up to Samuel Taylor Coleridge and, grasping his arm, begged him not to listen to the baleful woman because it would be their ruin, but he boldly advanced toward the woman and, bowing to her, declared himself ready to play. The woman handed him the dice cup and Samuel Taylor Coleridge took it and clasped it to his breast. Then he shook it furiously and threw the dice onto the table. The sailors gave a cheer: their captain had rolled an eleven. The baleful woman tore her hair and wept, then laughed malignly, then wept again, moaning like a whining dog. Finally, she took the dice and with a wide gesture as if her arm would sweep the bridge, she threw them down. The dice rolled onto the table and came to a stop, displaying six dots on one and six on the other. Just then, a freezing wind came up and covered them with icy gusts, and the sailors, the baleful woman, and the ship disappeared with the wind. A pall of gray smoke spread over everything and Samuel Taylor Coleridge opened his eyes to see a misty dawn outside his window.

DREAM OF GIACOMO LEOPARDI,
POET AND MOON-LOVER

One night on the first of December, in 1827, in the beautiful city of Pisa, on via della Faggiola, sleeping between two mattresses to protect himself from the terrible cold that was strangling the city, Giacomo Leopardi, poet and moon-lover, had a dream. He dreamed that he was in a desert and that he was a shepherd. But, instead of having a flock that followed him, he was comfortably seated on a buggy pulled by four white sheep, and those four sheep were his flock.

The desert and the hills that bordered it were of very fine silver sand that shone like the light of fireflies. It was night but it wasn't cold; rather, it seemed a beautiful night in late spring, so Leopardi removed the overcoat that covered him and laid it on the armrest of the buggy.

Where are you taking me, my dear little sheep? he asked.

We're taking you for a ride, answered the four sheep. We are little vagabond sheep.

But what is this place? asked Leopardi. Where are we?

Oh, you'll find out, answered the sheep, when you've met the person who is waiting for you.

Who is this person? asked Leopardi. I really want to know.

Ha ha, laughed the sheep, looking at one another. We can't tell you. It has to be a surprise.

Leopardi was hungry and would have liked to eat a sweet. A lovely cake with pine nuts is what he really wanted.

I'd like a sweet, he said. Isn't there a place where we could buy a sweet in this desert?

Right behind that hill, replied the little sheep, just be a bit patient.

They came to the end of the desert and circled the hill, at the foot of which was a shop. It was a beautiful pastry shop made entirely of crystal, and it sparkled with silver lights. Leopardi began looking in the window, not sure what to chose. In the first row were cakes of every color and every size: green pistachio cakes, vermilion raspberry cakes, yellow lemon cakes, pink strawberry cakes. Then there was marzipan, in comic, appetizing shapes: apples and oranges, cherries or small animals. And finally came the zabaiones, thick and creamy, with an almond on top. Leopardi called the baker and he bought three sweets: a strawberry cake, a marzipan, and a zabaione. The baker was a tiny man all in silver, with white hair and blue eyes, who gave him the sweets and a complimentary box of chocolates. Leopardi got back up on the buggy and, while the sheep were getting underway, he began sampling the delicacies he'd bought. The road had begun to climb, and now was twisting its way up the hill. And, how strange, even that terrain was shining, translucent, and emitting silver flashes. The little sheep stopped in front of a small house that was sparkling in the night. Giacomo Leopardi stepped down because he knew he had arrived, took the box of chocolates and entered the house. Inside, seated on a chair, was a girl embroidering on a hoop.

Come in, I've been waiting for you, said the girl. She turned and smiled at him, and Giacomo Leopardi recognized her. It was Sylvia. Only now she was completely silver, she had the same appearance as before but she was silver.

Sylvia, dear Sylvia, said Leopardi, taking her hands, how nice it is to see you again, but why are you all silver?

Because I am a little Selene. When you die you come to the moon and become like this.

But why am I here too? he asked. Could I be dead?

That you are not, Sylvia said. It's only an idea you have. You are still on earth.

And can you see the earth from here? Leopardi asked.

Sylvia led him to a window where there was a spyglass. Leopardi went up to the lens of the eyepiece and immediately saw a palace. He recognized it: it was his palace. A window was even lit up. Leopardi looked inside and saw his father, in his nightshirt with a chamber pot in hand; he was going to bed. He felt a sharp pang in his heart and he moved the spyglass. He saw a leaning tower in a large field and, nearby, a winding street and a palace where there was a faint glow.

He endeavored to look inside the window and saw a modest room, with a chest of drawers and a table on which there was a notebook, next to which was burning the stump of a candle. In the bed, he saw himself sleeping between two mattresses.

Am I dead? he asked Sylvia.

No, said Sylvia, you are only sleeping and you are dreaming of the moon.

DREAM OF CARLO COLLODI, WRITER AND THEATER CENSOR

The night of December 25, 1882, in his house in Florence, Carlo Collodi, writer and theater censor, had a dream. He dreamed that he was on a little paper boat in the middle of the sea and that there was a storm. But the little paper boat resisted, it was a stubborn little boat, with two human eyes and flying the Italian colors, which Collodi loved. From the coastal cliffs a far-off voice cried: Carlino, Carlino, come back to shore! It was the voice of the wife he had never had, a sweet feminine voice that called him with the cry of a siren.

Oh, how he wished he could go back! But he couldn't do it, the waves were too big and the little boat was sailing along at the mercy of the sea.

Then, all of a sudden, he saw the monster. It was an enormous shark with wide-open jaws, and it was looking suspiciously at him, studying him, waiting for him.

Collodi tried to work the rudder, but even the rudder was made of paper and it was completely soaked, by now it had become useless. And so he resigned himself to gliding directly into the jaws of the monster and because he was frightened he put his hands over his eyes, stood up, and shouted: Long live Italy!

How dark it was in the monster's belly! Collodi began to walk blindly, stumbling over something, he knew not what, and, touching it with his hands, he discovered it was a skull. Then he bumped into some planks and he knew that another boat before him had been shipwrecked in the jaws of the monster. Now he was moving easier because a dim gleam of light was coming from the open mouth of the shark. Walking ahead blindly, he hit his knee against a wooden crate. He bent over and touched it, and realized that it was filled with candles. Luckily, he still had his flintstone, with which he promptly struck a spark. He lit two candles and with those in hand he began to look around. He was on the deck of a vessel that had been shipwrecked in the belly of the monster. The quarter-deck was awash with skeletons, and a black flag with skull and crossbones fluttered on the mainmast. Collodi went on and climbed down a small ladder. He immediately found the galley, which was full of rum. With great satisfaction he opened a bottle and gulped it down. Now he felt better. Much refreshed, he got up and, guiding himself by candlelight, he got off the vessel. The belly of the monster was slippery, full of small dead fish and crabs. Collodi moved forward, splashing in the shallow water. Far away, he saw a faint light, a pale gleam that was summoning him. He went toward it. Skeletons, shipwrecked vessels, sunken boats, huge dead fish passed nearby. The faint light drew closer, and a table glided past Collodi. Two people were seated at the table, a woman and a child.

Collodi advanced timidly, and saw that the woman had indigo hair and the child a hat made of bread crumbs. He ran to embrace them. They embraced him too, and he laughed as they stroked one another's cheeks, making myriad affectionate gestures. And they didn't say an word.

All of a sudden the scene changed. Now he was no longer in the belly of the monster, but under a pergola. Summer was in full flower. And they were seated around a table at a house in the hills of Pescia, the cicadas were humming, everything was stone-still in the midday heat, they were drinking white wine and eating melons. Seated on one side, under the pergola, were a cat and a fox who were looking at them with placid eyes. And Collodi said to them politely: Won't you join us?

DREAM OF ROBERT LOUIS STEVENSON, WRITER AND TRAVELER

One night in June, 1865, in a hospital room in Edinburgh when he was fifteen years old, Robert Louis Stevenson, future writer and traveler, had a dream. He dreamed he had become a mature man and that he was on a clipper ship. The ship's sails were full in the wind as it traveled through the air. He took the helm and guided the ship as if he were the pilot of an aerial balloon. The ship passed over Edinburgh, then crossed the French mountains, left Europe behind and began to sail over a blue ocean. He knew he had taken that ship because of his lungs that could not breath, and he needed air. And now he was breathing really well, the winds were filling his lungs with clean air and his cough was calmed.

The sailing ship settled on the water and began to move along swiftly. Robert Louis Stevenson unfurled all the sails and allowed the wind to lead. At a certain point he saw an island on the horizon and many long canoes steered by dark men coming to meet him. Robert Louis Stevenson saw that the canoes were drawing alongside and showing him the way to go; and while they were doing this, the natives were singing merry songs and placing wreaths of white flowers on the bridge of the ship.

When he had come within a few hundred yards of the island, Robert Louis Stevenson dropped anchor and descended a rope ladder into the main canoe, which was waiting for him under the bulwarks. It was a stately canoe, with a gigantic totem on the prow. The natives embraced him and fanned him with large palm leaves, while offering him the sweetest fruits.

Awaiting them on the island were women and children who were dancing and laughing, and placing wreaths of flowers around his neck. The village headman approached them and pointed to the summit of the mountain. Robert Louis Stevenson realized that he had to reach it, but he didn't know why. He thought that with his difficulty in breathing he would never be able to reach the top. And with imperfect signs he tried to explain this to the people. But they had already understood and had prepared a sedan chair woven of rushes and palm leaves. Robert Louis Stevenson made himself comfortable, and four robust men hoisted the sedan chair on their shoulders and began to climb the mountain. Ascending, Robert Louis Stevenson saw an inexplicable panorama: he saw Scotland and France, America and New York, and all his past life that must in some way still exist. And along the sides of the mountain beneficial trees and full-blown flowers filled the air with a perfume that opened his lungs.

The natives stopped in front of a grotto and sat down on the earth cross-legged. Robert Louis Stevenson understood that he had to enter the grotto. They gave him a torch and he went in. It was cool, and the air was musky. Robert Louis Stevenson walked into the heart of the mountain, into a natural chamber that ancient earthquakes had excavated in the rocks, and in which were enormous stalactites. There was a silver chest in the middle of the room. Robert Louis Stevenson opened it and saw that inside lay a book. It was a book about an island, journeys, adventures, about a boy and pirates; and his name was written on the book. So he went back to the grotto, gave orders to the natives to return to the village, and climbed up to the summit with the book under his arm. Then he stretched out on the grass and opened the book to the first page. He knew that he would stay there, on that mountain top, to read that book. The air was pure, and because the story was like the air, it opened up the soul. And it was a fine place to read and wait for the end.

DREAM OF ARTHUR RIMBAUD,
POET AND VAGABOND

The night of June 23, 1891, in the hospital in Marseilles, Arthur Rimbaud, poet and vagabond, had a dream. He dreamed that he was crossing the Ardennes. He carried his amputated leg under his arm and he was leaning on a crutch. The amputated leg was wrapped in a newspaper on which his poetry was printed in large type.

It was near midnight and there was a full moon. The fields were silver, and Arthur was singing. He arrived in the environs of a large farmhouse in which there was a lighted window. He stretched out in the meadow under an enormous almond tree and continued to sing. He sang a revolutionary, vagabond song about a woman and a gun. After a little while the door opened and a woman came forward. She was a young woman, and had flowing hair. If you want a gun, as your song asks, I can give it to you, said the woman. I have it in the barn.

Rimbaud held on to his amputated leg and laughed. I'm going to the Paris Commune, he said, and I need a gun.

The woman led him to the barn. It was a two-story building. There were sheep on the ground floor, and on the floor above, where the rungs of a stairway ascended, there was a granary. I can't go up there, said Rimbaud, I'll wait for you here, among the sheep. He lay down on the straw and took off his trousers. When the woman came back down, he was ready to make love. If you want a woman, as your song asks, said the woman, I can give her to you. Rimbaud embraced her and asked: What's this woman's name? She's called Aurelia, said the woman, because she is a dream woman. And she unfastened her dress.

They made love among the sheep, and Rimbaud kept his amputated leg very close by. After they'd made love, the woman said: Stay.

I can't, answered Rimbaud. I have to go. Come outside with me to watch the dawn come up. They went out into the clearing, already getting light. You don't hear these cries, said Rimbaud, but I hear them, they come from Paris and call to me. It's liberty, and the call of distance.

The woman was still naked under the almond tree. I'll leave my leg with you, said Rimbaud. Take care of it.

And he headed toward the main road. How wonderful, he wasn't limping anymore now. He walked as if he had two legs. And the street echoed under his sandals. The dawn was rosy on the horizon. He sang, and he was happy.

ANTON PAVLOVICH CHEKHOV,
WRITER AND DOCTOR

One night in 1890, while he was on the island of Sakhalin, where he had gone to visit the prisoners, Anton Chekhov, writer and doctor, had a dream. He dreamed he was in a hospital ward and that they had put him in a straightjacket. Next to him were two frail old men who were acting out their madness. He was awake, lucid, confident, and he would have liked to write a story about a horse. A doctor arrived, dressed in white, and Anton Chekhov asked him for pen and paper.

You cannot write because you're too theoretical, said the doctor, you're only a poor moralist—and the mad are not allowed to.

What's your name? Anton Chekhov asked him.

I can't tell you my name, replied the doctor, but you should know that I hate those who write, especially if they are too theoretical. Theory ruins the world.

Anton Chekhov had an urge to slap him, but meanwhile the doctor had taken out lipstick and was applying it to his lips. Then he put on a wig and said: I am your nurse, but you can't write, because you're too theoretical, you're only a moralist, and you went to Sakhalin in your nightclothes. And saying this, he let go of his arm.

You're a poor devil, said Anton Chekhov, but you don't know a thing about horses.

Why should I know about horses? asked the doctor, I know only the director of my hospital.

Your director is an ass, said Anton Chekhov. He's not a horse, he's a beast of burden, he has borne much in his life. And then he added, he makes me write.

You can't write, said the doctor, because you're crazy.

The old men next to him kept turning over in bed, and one of them got up to piss in the chamber pot.

Never mind, said Anton Chekhov, I'll give you a knife, you can put that between your teeth; and with that knife in your mouth you'll kiss your clinic director and exchange a kiss of steel.

Then he turned over on his side and began to think about a horse. And a driver. And the driver was unhappy because he wanted to tell someone about the death of his only male child. But no one would listen to him because people didn't have time and considered him a pest. And now the driver was telling his horse, who was a patient beast. He was an old horse that had human eyes.

And at that moment two winged horses arrived at a gallop, ridden by two women Anton Chekhov knew. They were two actresses, and they were holding a branch of flowering cherry in their hands. The driver hitched the two horses to his landau, Anton Chekhov settled into the seat and the carriage took off through the hospital ward, slipped through one of the big windows and soared off into the sky. And while they flew through the clouds they saw the doctor with the wig, who was making peevish gestures and inveighing against them. The two actresses scattered two cherry blossom petals and the driver smiled, saying: I'd have a story to tell. It's a sad story, but I believe you can understand me, dear Anton Chekhov.

Anton Chekhov leaned back on the seat, turned his scarf up around his neck and said: I have lots of time, I'm very patient, and I love people's stories.

DREAM OF ACHILLE-CLAUDE DEBUSSY,
MUSICIAN AND AESTHETE

The night of June 29, 1893, a limpid summer night, Achille-Claude Debussy, musician and aesthete, dreamed that he was on a beach. It was a beach in the Tuscan Maremma, bordered by low thickets and pines. Debussy arrived in linen trousers and a straw hat; he went into the cabana that Pinky had consigned him and took off his clothes. He glimpsed Pinky on the beach, but instead of acknowledging her with a greeting, he slipped into the shadow of the cabana. Owner of a villa, Pinky was a beautiful woman who attended to the rare bathers on her private beach and strolled on the seashore, covered by a blue veil that fell from her hat. She belonged to the old nobility and spoke to everyone with the familiar "tu." This did not please Debussy, who liked to be treated with formulas of courtesy.

Before putting on his bathing suit, he did some deep knee bends, and then stroked his half-erect penis a long time, because the vision of that solitary beach, with the sun and the blue of the sea, was rather arousing. He put on his austere bathing costume, blue, with two white stars on the back. Just then, he saw that Pinky — she and her two Great Danes, who always accompanied her — had disappeared, and there was no one on the beach. Debussy crossed the beach with a bottle of champagne he had brought with him. Arriving at the water's edge, he dug a small hole in the sand and slipped the bottle into it to keep it chilled, then entered the sea and swam.

He immediately felt the beneficent influence of the water. He loved the sea more than anything, and would have liked to dedicate some music to it. The sun was at the zenith and the surface of the water was sparkling. Debussy swam back to shore with long calm strokes. When he reached the beach, he dug out the bottle of champagne and drank about half of it. It seemed to him that time had stopped and he thought that music should do this: stop time.

He set out toward the cabana and undressed. While he was undressing he heard noises in the thicket and turned around. In the bushes, a few yards in front of him, he saw a faun who was courting two nymphs. One nymph was caressing the faun's shoulders, while the other, with heavy languor, made dance movements.

Debussy felt a great lassitude and began to caress himself languidly. Then he walked toward the thicket. When they saw him come, the three beings smiled at him and the faun began to play a flute. It was exactly the music that Debussy would have wanted to compose, and he registered it mentally. Then he sat down on the pine needles, his penis erect. Now the faun took a nymph and clasped her tight. And the other nymph approached Debussy with lissome dance steps and caressed his belly. It was afternoon, and time stood still.

DREAM OF HENRI DE TOULOUSE-LAUTREC, PAINTER AND UNHAPPY MAN

One March night in 1890, in a Paris brothel, after having painted a poster for a dancer whom he loved without reciprocation, Henri de Toulouse-Lautrec, painter and unhappy man, had a dream. He dreamed that he was in the countryside of his Albi, and that it was summer. He was under a cherry tree full of cherries and he wished he could pick some, but his short and deformed legs didn't allow him to reach the first branch loaded with fruit. So, he stood on tiptoes and, as if it were the most natural thing in the world, his legs began to grow longer until they reached normal length. After he had picked the cherries, his legs began to grow short again, and Henri de Toulouse-Lautrec resumed his dwarfish height.

Well, he exclaimed, so I can grow at my pleasure. And he felt happy. He began to cross a wheat field. Spikes of grain towered over him and his head opened a furrow through the vegetation. It seemed to him that he was in a strange forest where he was making his way blindly. At the end of the field was a brook. Henri de Toulouse-Lautrec looked at himself in it and he saw an ugly dwarf with deformed legs wearing checkered trousers and a hat on his head. Then he stood on tiptoes and his legs grew gently longer. He became a normal man and the water reflected an image of a handsome and elegant young man.

Once again, Henri de Toulouse-Lautrec grew short, he undressed and immersed himself in the brook to cool off. When he had bathed, he dried himself in the sun, dressed again, and set off on his way. Night was falling, and at the end of the plain he saw a crown of lights. He capered toward it on his short legs and when he got there he realized that he was in Paris. It was the Moulin Rouge building, with its illuminated windmill blades turning on the roof. A large crowd was milling around the entrance, and near the box office a large poster in flashy colors announced the evening's performance, a can-can. The poster pictured a dancer with skirts raised, who danced downstage facing the gas footlights. Henri de Toulouse-Lautrec was pleased, because the poster had been painted by him. Then he avoided mixing with the crowd and entered by the side door through a poorly illuminated passageway and made his way into the wings. The performance had just begun. The music was riotous and Jane Avril, on stage, was dancing like a demon. Henri de Toulouse-Lautrec felt a wild desire to go up on the stage himself and to take Jane Avril by the hand and dance with her. He stood on tiptoes and his legs grew longer at once. Then he threw himself into the dance with fervor, his top hat fell to one side and he let himself be swept up by the whirlwind of the can-can. Jane Avril did not seem at all surprised that he had attained a normal stature, she danced and sang and embraced him, and she was happy. And then the curtain fell, the stage disappeared, and Henri de Toulouse-Lautrec was once again with his Jane Avril in the countryside of Albi. Now it was high noon again and the cicadas were humming crazily. Jane Avril, exhausted from the heat and the dance, fell to the ground beneath an oak tree and drew her skirts up to her knees. Then she opened her arms to Henri de Toulouse-Lautrec and he surrendered himself to her in pleasure. Jane Avril held him to her breast and cradled him as if cradling a baby. I liked you with short legs too, she whispered in his ear, but now that your legs have grown, I like you even more. Henri de Toulouse-Lautrec smiled and embraced her in his turn, and hugging the pillow, he turned on his side and continued to dream.

DREAM OF FERNANDO PESSOA,
POET AND PRETENDER

On the night of March 7, 1914, Fernando Pessoa, poet and pretender, dreamed he was waking up. He had coffee in his small rented room, shaved and got dressed in elegant fashion. He put on his raincoat because it was raining outside. It was twenty minutes to eight when he left, and at eight sharp he was at the central station, on the platform of the direct train to Santarém. The train left with the utmost promptness, at 8:05. Fernando Pessoa took a seat in a compartment in which was seated a lady apparently about fifty, who was reading. She was his mother but she was not his mother, and she was immersed in her reading. Fernando Pessoa began to read too. That day he had to read two letters that had reached him from South Africa and that spoke to him of his distant childhood.

The lady apparently about fifty said, at a certain point, I was like grass and they didn't pull me up. Fernando Pessoa liked the phrase and jotted it down in a notebook. Meanwhile, the flat Ribatejan countryside of rice fields and grasslands passed in front of them. When they reached Santarém, Fernando Pessoa took a carriage. Do you know the whereabouts of a solitary whitewashed house? he asked the driver.

The driver was a tiny fat fellow, with a nose reddened by alcohol. Of course, he said, it is Senhor Caeiro's house, I know it well. And he whipped the horse. The horse began to trot down the main road lined with palm trees. In the fields straw huts were visible, with black men at the doors.

But where are we? Pessoa asked the driver. Where are you taking me?

We are in South Africa, answered the driver, and I am taking you to Senhor Caeiro's house

Pessoa felt reassured and leaned back in the seat. Ah, so he was in South Africa, that was what he really wanted. He crossed his legs in a satisfied manner and saw his naked calves, in two navy-blue trouser legs. He realized that he was a child and this delighted him very much. It was wonderful to be a child who was traveling through South Africa. He took out a package of cigarettes and he lit one with pleasure. He also offered one to the driver, who eagerly accepted.

Twilight was falling when they came in view of a white house on a hill punctuated with cypresses. It was a typical house of the Ribatejo, long and low, with sloping red tiles. The carriage entered the avenue of cypresses, the gravel crunched under the wheels, a dog barked in the fields.

At the door of the house was an elderly woman wearing glasses and a white bonnet. Pessoa understood immediately that this was Alberto Caeiro's great aunt, and rising on tiptoes he kissed her cheek.

Don't tire my dear Alberto too much, said the old woman. He is in delicate health.

She stepped aside and Pessoa went into the house. It consisted of a single ample room, furnished simply. There was a little fireplace, a small bookcase, a sideboard full of plates, a sofa and two armchairs. Alberto Caeiro was seated in an armchair, his head resting on the back. It was headmaster Nicholas, Pessoa's high school teacher.

I didn't know that Caeiro was you, said Fernando Pessoa, and made a small bow. With a weary nod, he motioned for Fernando Pessoa to come forward. Come here, dear Pessoa, he said, I've called you here because I wanted you to know the truth.

Meanwhile, the great aunt came in with a tray of tea and cookies. Caeiro and Pessoa served themselves and enjoyed a cup. Pessoa remembered not to raise his little finger, because it wasn't elegant. He straightened the collar of his sailor suit and lit a cigarette. You are my master, he said.

Caeiro sighed, and then smiled. It's a long story, he said, but it's fruitless to explain it to you from the beginning. You are intelligent and will understand even if I skip over some parts. You should know only this, that I am you.

Explain yourself better, said Pessoa.

I am the deepest side of you, said Caeiro, your dark side. In this I am your master.

From the bell tower in the neighboring village the hour struck.

And what should I do? asked Pessoa.

You must follow my voice, said Caeiro. You will listen to me in waking and in sleep. Sometimes I'll disturb you, and sometimes you won't want to hear me. But you must listen to me, you must have the courage to listen to this voice if you want to be a great poet.

I'll do it, said Pessoa. I promise you.

He rose and took his leave. The carriage was waiting for him at the door. Now he had become an adult again and his mustache had grown back. Where should I take you? asked the driver. Take me toward the end of the dream, said Pessoa, today is the triumphant day of my life.

It was March eighth, and into Pessoa's window filtered a pale sun.

DREAM OF VLADIMIR MAYAKOVKSY,
POET AND REVOLUTIONARY

In 1930, on the third of April, in the last month of his life, Vladimir Mayakovsky, poet and revolutionary, had the same dream he had now been dreaming every night for a year.

He dreamed he was in the Moscow subway, on a train that was moving at an insane speed. He was fascinated by the speed, because he loved the future and machines, but now he felt anxious to get off the train and he insistently kept turning an object he held in his pocket. To calm his anxiety he thought he'd sit down, and he chose a seat near on old woman dressed in black, who was carrying a shopping bag. When Mayakovsky sat down next to her she jumped up in terror.

Am I so ugly? thought Mayakovsky, and smiled at the old woman. Meanwhile, he told her, don't be afraid, I'm only a cloud and don't want anything except to get off this train.

Finally, the train stopped at a station somewhere, and Mayakovsky got off without being noticed. He went into the first restroom he found and took the object out of his pocket. It was a bar of yellow soap, the kind laundresses use. He turned on the faucet and began to scrub his hands carefully, but the dirt he felt on his palms wouldn't come off. Then he put the soap back into his pocket and went out into the atrium. The station was deserted. In the back, under a large poster, were three men who came to meet him as soon as they saw him. They wore black raincoats and felt hats.

Political police, the three men said in unison. Security search.

Mayakovsky raised his arms and let himself be searched.

And what's this? asked one of the men in a contemptuous way, waving the bar of soap.

I don't know, Mayakovsky said fiercely. I don't know anything about these things. I'm only a cloud.

This is soap, the man who was interrogating him whispered insidiously, and you certainly wash your hands often enough. The soap is still wet.

Mayakovsky didn't answer and wiped his forehead, which was bathed in sweat.

Come with us, said the man, who took his arm while the other two followed them.

They went up a stairway and came out into a big open-air station. Below the station was a tribunal, with judges in military garb and an audience of children dressed like small orphans.

The three men led him up to the bench of the accused and gave the soap to one of the judges. The judge took a megaphone and said: Our security forces caught the accused in flagrante delicto. He was still carrying this evidence of his suspicious activities in his pocket.

The audience of orphans let forth a chorus of disapproval.

The accused is condemned to the locomotive, said the judge, striking the bench with his wooden gavel.

Two guards came forward, stripping Mayakovsky and dressing him in an enormous yellow smock. Then they led him toward a puffing locomotive, driven by a half-naked engine stoker who had a feral appearance. A hangman wearing a hangman's hood was on the locomotive, and he was holding a lash in his hand.

Now we'll see what you can do, said the hangman, and the locomotive departed.

Mayakovsky looked outside and was aware that they were crossing Great Russia — immense fields and vast plains, where emaciated men and women lay prostrate on the earth with their wrists bound.

These people are waiting for your poems, said the hangman. Sing, poet! And he whipped him.

Mayakovsky began to recite his worst poems. They were thunderous poems, ceremonial poems, rhetorical poems. And while he recited them, the people raised their fists and cursed him and cursed his mother.

Then Vladimir Mayakovsky woke up and went to the bathroom to wash his hands.

DREAM OF FEDERICO GARCIA LORCA, POET AND ANTI-FASCIST

One August night in 1936, in his house in Granada, Federico García Lorca had a dream. He dreamed he was on the stage of his traveling theater and, accompanying himself on the piano, he was singing a Gypsy song. He wore tails, but had on his head a *mazantini* with a broad brim. His audience was composed of old women dressed in black with mantillas over their shoulders, listening, enraptured. A voice from the hall requested a song and Federico García Lorca began to perform it. It was a song about duels and orange groves, passion and death. When he had finished singing, Federico García Lorca stood up and bowed to his public. The curtain came down and only then did he realize that there was no scenic backdrop behind the piano, but that the theater opened out into empty fields. It was night and there was a moon. Federico García Lorca looked between the panels of the curtain and saw that the theater had emptied out as if by magic. The hall was completely deserted and the lights were dimming. At that moment he heard a yelp; and running along behind him was a small black dog that seemed to be waiting for him. Federico García Lorca felt compelled to follow it and took a step forward. The dog, as if by a prearranged signal, began to trot along very slowly, leading the way. Where are you taking me, little black dog? Federico García Lorca asked. The dog whined piteously and Federico García Lorca shuddered. He turned and saw that behind him the canvas and wooden walls of his theater had disappeared. In the moonlight there remained a deserted orchestra pit, while the piano, as if invisible fingers were touching the keys, continued to play an ancient melody all by itself. The field was divided by a wall—a long, useless white wall, beyond which one could see another field. The dog stopped and whined again, and Federico García Lorca stopped too. Then soldiers filed out from behind the wall and surrounded him, laughing. They were dressed in brown shirts and wore three-cornered hats on their heads. They each held a rifle in one hand, and a bottle of wine in the other. Their commander was a monstrous dwarf, his head covered with warts. You are a traitor, said the dwarf, and we are your executioners. Federico García Lorca spat in his face while the soldiers held him fast. The dwarf laughed obscenely and shouted to the soldiers to cut off his pants. You are a female, he said, and females must not wear pants, they must stay shut up in the rooms of their houses and cover their heads with mantillas. At a nod from the dwarf, the soldiers tied Lorca up, cut off his pants, and covered his head with a shawl. Filthy female who dresses like a man, said the dwarf, the time has come for you to pray to the Holy Virgin. Federico García Lorca spat in his face, and the dwarf wiped it off, laughing. Then he took the pistol from his pocket and stuck the barrel into Lorca's mouth.

The piano melody drifted over the fields. The dog whined. Federico García Lorca heard a shot and sat bolt upright up in bed. They were rapping at the door of his house in Granada with the butt of a rifle.

DREAM OF SIGMUND FREUD,
INTERPRETER OF OTHER PEOPLE'S DREAMS

On the night of the twenty-second of September in 1939, the day before he died, Dr. Sigmund Freud, interpreter of other people's dreams, had a dream.

He dreamed he had become Dora, and that he was crossing a bombarded Vienna. The city was destroyed, and dust and smoke were rising from the ruins of the palaces.

How is it possible that this city was destroyed? Dr. Freud asked himself, and he tried to stabilize his newly acquired breasts. But just then, on the Rathausstrasse, he ran into Frau Marta who was coming toward him, holding out a copy of the *Neue Frei Presse*.

Oh, dear Dora, said Frau Marta, I just read that Dr. Freud has returned to Vienna from Paris, and he's living right here at number seven Rathuasstrasse. Maybe it would do you good to see him. And, that said, she nudged aside the corpse of a soldier with her foot.

Dr. Freud felt deeply ashamed, and lowered his veil. I don't understand why, he said timidly.

Because you have so many problems, dear Dora, said Frau Marta. You have so many problems as we all do. You need to confide in someone and, believe me, there's no one better than Dr. Freud for confidences. He understands everything about women—sometimes he really seems to be a woman, since he identifies so with their role.

Dr. Freud took his leave, kindly but quickly, and he went on his way. A little farther on he ran into the butcher boy, who stared hard at him, appraising him intently. Dr. Freud stopped, because he wanted to fight him, but the butcher boy was looking at his legs and said: Dora, you need a real man, instead of being in love with your fantasies.

Irritated, Dr. Freud stopped. And you, how do you know? he asked.

Everyone in Vienna knows, said the butcher boy. You have too many sexual fantasies. As Dr. Freud discovered.

Dr. Freud raised his fists. This was too much. That he, Dr. Freud, had sexual fantasies! It was the others who had these fantasies, those who came to confide in him. He was a man of the highest integrity, and that kind of fantasy was a problem of children or disturbed people.

Don't be an idiot, laughed the butcher boy, touching him lightly.

Dr. Freud perked up. After all, it was rather agreeable to be treated familiarly by a sexy butcher boy, and, after all, he was Dora, who had sordid sexual problems.

He went along Rathausstrasse and came to his own house. His house, his beautiful house, no longer existed; it had been destroyed by shelling. But in the small garden, which had survived intact, was his couch. And on the couch lay a young lout wearing clogs and an open shirt. He was snoring.

Dr. Freud approached and woke him up. What are you doing? he asked. The young lout stared at him wide-eyed. I'm looking for Dr. Freud, he said.

I am Dr. Freud, said Dr. Freud.

Don't make me laugh, Fraulein, replied the young lout.

Well, said Dr. Freud, I'll confess something: today I decided to assume the guise of one of my patients, and that's why I'm dressed like this. I'm Dora.

Dora, said the young lout. But I love you. And saying this, he put his arms around Dr. Freud. Dr. Freud felt deeply bewildered but let himself fall back onto the couch. And at this moment he awakened. It was his last night, but he didn't know it.

Daedalus
Architect and first aviator, perhaps he is one of our dreams.

Publius Ovidus Naso
Born in Sulmona in 42 BC. Ovid grew up in Rome, where he studied rhetoric and took on various public duties. He was a great poet, provided with a superb Hellenistic education, and in the *Metamorphoses* he sang the apotheosis of Augustus, describing his transformation into a star. But his career, perhaps because of a court scandal in which he was implicated, was interrupted by an imperial decree that banished him to Tomi, on the Black Sea. In Tomi, Ovid died in solitude, in 18 AD, in spite of supplications sent to Augustus and to his successor, Tiberius.

Lucius Apuleius
125–180 AD. Born in Madaura, in North Africa, he studied rhetoric in Carthage, Rome, and Athens, and was initiated into the mystery cults. He married the widow Prudentilla and was accused by her relatives of having used diabolical arts to press her into marriage in order to gain possession of her dowry. His books reveal a mysterious, mystical man, inclined to esotericism. His best-known book, *The Golden Ass*, is a kind of initiatory biography, which narrates the vicissitudes of the young Lucius, changed into an ass by magic, who finally regains his human form.

Cecco Angioliere
Sienna, 1260–1310. An irascible and blasphemous Tuscan, he was tried and fined. He squandered his inheritance and died in misery. While the poetry of his time celebrated the angelic woman, he sang the praises of the nag daughter of a tanner. He

was a specialist in vituperation and insults, and he wrote about gambling, wine, money, hatred of his parents, and the damnation of the world.

François Villon

Born in 1431, the date of his death is uncertain. His real name was François de Montcorbier, and he assumed the name of his tutor, who was like a father to him. He led a disordered and turbulent life, killed a priest in a brawl, took part in robbery and looting. He was sentenced to death, a sentence then commuted to exile. He celebrated in his ballads the jargon of the underworld he frequented, and in his *Testament* he wrote of love and death, hatred, poverty, hunger, the underworld, repentance.

François Rabelais

1444–1553. He was a Dominican friar, left the order, and became a famous doctor at a Lyons hospital. But he never gave up the practices of monastic life. He was a learned Latinist and was disliked by the authorities of his time because of his progressive ideas. Perhaps to sublimate the fasts that his monastic rules imposed on him, he wrote a book that is still famous, inventing two giants, Gargantua and Pantagruel, who are the greatest eaters and jovial spirits in all Western literature.

Michelangelo Merisi, called Caravaggio

Caravaggio, 1573–Porto Ercole, 1610. From his native region he went to Rome, where he lived in sad misery until he was noticed by the Cavaliere d'Arpino, who gave him his first work. After taking his own measure in still life painting, he began to create great religious and dramatic canvases in his inimitable chiaroscuro. *The Calling of St. Matthew* is perhaps his masterpiece. He was a man quick to use fists and knives. He committed murder in a brawl, fled to Naples and then to Malta, where he was imprisoned, then managed to escape. Pursued by assassins, he landed in Porto Ercole, where he died of fever.

Francisco Goya y Lucientes

Saragossa, 1746–Bordeaux, 1828. Born poor and died poor. He studied painting in Madrid, traveled to Italy, visiting Rome and Venice. At the Spanish courts he knew fame and misfortune, seductive success and searing bitterness. The Duchess of Alba protected him, and he immortalized her in his paintings. He was afflicted by sporadic madness. His *Capriccios*, drawn in 1799, cost him a trial before the Inquisition. He portrayed terrifying visions, the disasters of war and the misfortunes of humankind.

Samuel Taylor Coleridge

1772–1834. Studied at Cambridge, but did not earn a degree. After a disappointment in love, he enlisted in a cavalry regiment under the false name of Silas Tomkyn Comberbach, and was ransomed out by money from his brother. He was a man who yearned for utopia: he was unitarian in religion and the founder of Pantosocracy, a communistic project aiming to free human beings from inequality. Through opium, which attracted him, he knew artificial paradises, but, unlike his friend De Quincey, he never boasted about his habit and practiced it in solitude. Visionary, dreamer, and metaphysician, he left us, among other things, a powerful delirium in ballad form, "The Rime of the Ancient Mariner."

Giacomo Leopardi

Recanati, 1798–1837. Born into a noble family, he studied voraciously in his father's library—sciences, philosophy, classical languages—but he grew up unhappy in body and spirit. He disliked the provincial prison in which he was raised, hated narrow-mindedness and pettiness, loved science, art, enlightened thought, and civic passion. He was a notable philologist, a bitter philosopher, and a lofty poet. He wrote about love, fleeting time, human unhappiness, the infinite, and the moon.

Carlo Collodi

His real name was Carlo Lorenzini, and he was born in Collodi, in Tuscany, in 1826, and died in Florence in 1890. He was a man of fervent Mazzinian ideas, participated in the military campaigns of the Risorgimento, and loved liberty and independence; yet he had to work from 1850 on as a theater censor in the Tuscan government. He was a gruff, solitary man given to excess in food and wine. He suffered from rheumatism, mania, and insomnia. With *Pinocchio*, he gave immortal life to a wooden puppet.

Robert Louis Stevenson

He was born in Edinburgh in 1850. In precarious health, his youth was consigned to long illnesses and interminable periods of convalescence. He suffered from lung ailments and died of tuberculosis. He traveled in Europe, the United States, and the Pacific. *Treasure Island* is his most celebrated book. He chose to die on a remote island, Upolu, in the Samoas, where he was buried on a mountain top. He was forty-four years old.

Arthur Rimbaud

Charleville, 1845–Marseilles, 1891. Born into an oppressive, bigoted, and conservative family, he fled to Paris at the age of fifteen to participate in the Commune, and began a stormy and disordered life, full of wanderings and adventures. He loved the poet Paul Verlaine, who shot him with a revolver in a fight. He endured disgrace and hospitalization. He traveled through Europe with a circus. After abandoning poetry, he was a smuggler in Abyssinia. He returned to France because of a tumor in a knee, had the leg amputated, and died in a Marseilles hospital.

Anton Pavlovich Chekov

1860–1904. Russian writer and playwright. He was a doctor, but practiced the profession only during famines and epidemics. He was ill with tuberculosis. In 1890 he crossed Siberia to reach the remote island of Sakhalin, site of a penal colony, and wrote a book about the terrible conditions of the prisoners. He loved a theater actress. He wrote short stories, dramas, and comedies. He wrote about daily life, ordinary people, the poor, children, and the great small things of life.

Claude-Achille Debussy

Saint-Germain-en-Laye, 1862–Paris 1918. He studied with maestros Marmontel and Guiraud, won the Prize of Rome, and spent three years at the Villa Medici. At first, he was enthusiastic about Wagner's music, but later lost his enthusiasm. He discovered Oriental music, which influenced him, at the Universal Exposition in Paris. He loved the symbolists, impressionists, decadents. He led a life of elegance and seclusion, devoted only to music and art.

Henri de Toulouse-Lautrec

Albi, 1864–Malromé, 1901. Descended from an ancient and noble French family, he was a painter, designer, and lithographer. Deformed in body, he led an unhappy, disorderly, and stormy existence in Paris, frequenting taverns, music halls, and whorehouses. He hated schools and academies. He painted clowns, actors, ballerinas, drunks, prostitutes, vice, misery, and loneliness.

Fernando Pessoa

Lisbon, 1888–1935. When he was a young boy his father died; and he was educated in South Africa, where his stepfather was the Portuguese Consul. He always had the consciousness of being a genius and the fear of becoming mad, as had his maternal grandmother. He knew he was plural, and accepted this fact in his writing and in his life, giving voice to many different poets, his "heteronyms," the master of whom was Alberto Caeiro, a man in delicate health who lived with an old great aunt in a country house in the Ribatejo. He spent his life as an employee in an import-export firm, translating commercial letters. He lived for the most part in modest rented rooms. He had only one love in his life, a brief and intense relationship, with Ophélia Queiroz, who was employed as a secretary in the firm where he worked. The "triumphant day" of his life was the eighth of March, when the poets who inhabited him began to write with his hand.

Vladimir Mayakovsky

Born in a village in Georgia in 1893, he studied painting, architecture, and sculpture. When he was very young, he joined the clandestine Bolshevik party and spent time in prison. Won over by the ideas of modernity, he soon became the coryphaeus of Futurism and, dressed in an orange smock, took a trip across Russia by train. He was an enthusiastic adherent of the Bolshevik revolution and held important posts in the revolutionary art world. He was an organizer, propagandist, designer of posters, and author of fervent and heroic poetry. In 1925 he published an unfortunate little celebratory poem about Lenin. But times were changing in his country, making difficulties for avant-garde artists. Disappointed and frightened, he was struck by a severe type of obsessive neurosis. He continually washed his hands, and always left the house with a bar of soap in his pocket. The official version holds that in 1930 he committed suicide with a pistol.

Federico García Lorca

Born in the province of Granada, in 1898, he studied in Madrid and was friend to the major artists of his generation. He was a poet, but also a musician, painter, and playwright. In 1932 the government of the Spanish Republic entrusted him with the task of creating a theater troupe that brought the classics to public awareness. Thus was born "La Baraca," a kind of caravan of thespians with which García Lorca toured all of Spain. In 1936 he founded an association of anti-fascist intellectuals. In *Cante Jondo* and in almost all of his poetry, he celebrated the traditions of Andalusian Gypsies, their songs and their passions. In 1936 he was assassinated near Granada by Francoist police.

Sigmund Freud

Freiberg, 1856–London 1939. He was a neurologist. He first studied hysteria and hypnotism with Charcot, then he interpreted the dreams of humankind (*The Interpretation of Dreams*, 1900), intending to extricate us from the unhappiness that plagues us. He maintained that people have inside themselves a dark knot he called the Unconscious. His *Case Histories* can be read as ingenious novels. Id, Ego, and Superego are his Trinity. And, perhaps, ours too.

The Last Three Days
of Fernando Pessoa

A Delirium

NOVEMBER 28, 1935

First, I must shave, he said. I don't want to go to the hospital unshaven. Please, go call the barber. He's Senhor Manacés, he lives at the corner.

But there's no time, Senhor Pessoa, the concierge replied. The taxi is already at the door, your friends have arrived and they're waiting for you in the lobby.

It doesn't matter, he replied, there's always time.

He settled into the chair where Senhor Manacés customarily gave him a shave, and began to read the poems of Sá-Carneiro.

Senhor Manacés came in and wished everyone a good evening. Senhor Pessoa, he said, they told me you're not feeling well. I hope it's nothing serious.

He wrapped a towel around Pessoa's neck and began to lather his face.

Tell me something, said Pessoa, you know so many interesting stories, Senhor Manacés, and see so many people in your shop. Tell me something.

Pessoa put on a dark suit that he'd recently had tailored for him, tied his bow tie, put on his glasses. It wasn't cold, but it was raining outside. So he put on his yellow overcoat, took a pen and notebook, and began to go downstairs.

Halfway down, he met his friends, Francisco Gouveia and Armando Teixeira Rebelo. They looked worried and held dripping umbrellas in their hands. We'll come with you, they both said at the same time. Pessoa smiled distractedly. He felt a sharp pain in his right side and it prevented him from being cordial. The two friends offered him an arm to help him downstairs, but he didn't accept and held onto the banister. In the lobby he saw his boss, Senhor Moitinho de Almeida, who was talking with the taxi driver. I'm coming too, Senhor Pessoa, Moitinho de Almeida said quickly. I'd prefer to come too, I can't let you go like this.

Don't trouble yourself, Senhor Moitinho de Almeida, replied Pessoa in a whisper. I already have two friends who are coming with me, please, don't trouble yourself.

But Senhor Moitinho de Almeida seemed determined. He opened the front door, Pessoa got in next to the driver, and his three companions settled into the back seat.

Riding in the cab, he gazed at length through the window at the cupola of the Estrela basilica. The basilica was beautiful, with that grand baroque dome and ornate façade. It was there in front, in the garden, that many years earlier he used to meet Ophélia Queiroz, his one and only love. On the bench in the Estrela garden they exchanged shy kisses and solemn promises to love each other forever.

But my life was stronger than I, stronger than my love, Pessoa murmured. Forgive me, Ophélia, but I had to write, had to write and nothing else. I couldn't do otherwise. Now it's all over.

The taxi passed in front of Parliament and then turned into Calçada do Combro. He'd once lived in that neighborhood, many years before, in a rented room. Dona Maria das Virtudes was the proprietor. He remembered her well. She was a buxom woman of sixty with bleached blonde hair who invited him evenings to drink her cherry liqueur and to participate in her spiritual seances. She made contact with her dead husband, Warrant Officer Pereira, and had long conversations with him about the African war and about the price of green peppers. Then they drank a little glass of *ginjinha,* ate a brandied cherry, and Pessoa took his leave: Good night Dona Maria das Virtudes, and sweet dreams. He retired to his room. On those nights he was in contact with Bernardo Soares and wrote under that name *The Book of Disquiet.*

He used to wake at dawn to see the gradations of light changing color over Lisbon and record them in a small leather-covered notebook that his mother had sent him from South Africa.

When they came to Rua Luz Soriano they were stopped by a policeman. You can't go through, said the policeman. The street has been taken over by a nationalist demonstration, there's a band and everything. The city is celebrating today.

Senhor Moitinho de Almeida leaned out of the window. I am Dr. Moitinho de Almeida, he said with authority. We have to get to the São Luís dos Franceses clinic, we have a sick man on board.

The policeman took off his cap and scratched his head. Look, senhor, he said, I'll let you make a small detour. It's a one-way street, but just this once you can go on through. Turn right here, then take a left and you'll be in the Bairro Alto. Pessoa smiled because he had recognized him. It was Coelho Pacheco, one of his rare heteronyms who had written poetry only once, and had written a dark and visionary poem in neo-gothic style. What was Coelho Pacheco doing dressed as a policeman? Perhaps the Master had sent him so that he might prepare the way. Pessoa raised his hand and gave him an eso-teric sign. Coelho Pacheco reciprocated with an esoteric sign, and the taxi took the first street to the right.

A nurse was dozing at the hospital reception desk. Senhor Moitinho de Almeida spoke to her, asked for the doctor on duty, said that it was urgent.

Pessoa sat down in an armchair and began to dream. He saw scenes from his childhood and heard the voice of his grand-mother Dionísia, who had died in a madhouse. Fernando, his grandmother said to him, you will be like me, because blood will tell, and all your life you will have me for company because life is madness and you will know how to live this madness.

Come with me, said the doctor, and took Pessoa's arm to support him. He led him into an examining room where there was a narrow bed and a strong odor of disinfectant. Get undressed, the doctor ordered. Pessoa got undressed. Lie down, the doctor ordered. Pessoa lay down. The doctor began to examine him, palpating his body. When he reached the upper part of his liver, Pessoa groaned. How long have you been feeling ill? the doctor asked. Since this afternoon, Pessoa replied. And what symptoms have you had? asked the doctor. Great pain, Pessoa answered, and green vomit.

The doctor called the nurse and said to put the patient in room number four. Then he took the register and wrote on the clinic card, "hepatic crisis."

Pessoa said goodbye to his friends. Senhor Moitinho de Almeida would have liked to stay, but Pessoa gently dismissed him. He gave the other two a quick embrace. Leave me, dear friends, he said; tonight and tomorrow I shall probably have visitors. Let's meet the day after tomorrow.

The room was a small, simple room, with an iron bed, a white dresser, and a small table. Pessoa got into bed, turned on the light on the night table, lowered his head onto the pillow and passed his hand over his right side. Fortunately, the pain had subsided now. The nurse brought him a glass of water and a compress, then she said: Excuse me, but I have to give you a shot. Doctor's orders.

Pessoa asked for a dose of laudanum, a sedative he used to take when, as Bernardo Soares, he couldn't get to sleep. The nurse brought it to him and Pessoa drank it. My name is Catarina, said the nurse. When you need anything, ring the bell and I'll come at once.

~ 2

What time is it? Pessoa asked.

Almost midnight, Álvaro de Campos answered, the best time to meet you. It's the hour of phantoms.

Why have you come? asked Pessoa.

Because if you are going away, we have some things to say to each other, replied Álvaro de Campos. I won't survive you. I'm leaving with you, but before we plumb the darkness we have some things to say to each other.

Pessoa raised up on his pillows, drank a sip of water, and asked: What have you done now?

My dear, answered Álvaro de Campos, I note with pleasure that you don't call me "Engineer," and that you don't address me formally. You treat me familiarly.

Certainly, Pessoa replied. You came into my life, you took me over, you put an end to my relationship with Ophélia.

I did it for your own good, replied Álvaro de Campos. That emancipated girl couldn't be good for a man of your age, it would have been a disastrous marriage. And then, you know, all those love letters you wrote her were ridiculous, so I protected you from ridicule. I really believe that all love letters are ridiculous. I hope you're grateful to me.

I loved her, Pessoa whispered.

With a ridiculous love, replied Álvaro de Campos.

Yes, of course, that's possible, answered Pessoa. And you?

I? said Campos. I, well, I have my irony, I wrote a sonnet that I've never shown you. It's about a love that will embarrass you because it's dedicated to a young man, a young man I loved and who loved me in England. So, after this sonnet, a legend of your repressed love will be born, and for some critics that will be sheer happiness.

Did you really love someone? Pessoa said softly.

I really loved someone, Álvaro de Campos replied in a low voice.

Then I absolve you, said Pessoa, I absolve you. I thought that in your life you'd loved only theory.

No, said Álvaro de Campos, moving closer to the bed. I also loved life, and if in my wild Futurist odes I wrote humbug, if in my nihilist poetry I destroyed everything, even myself, you should know that in my life I also loved, with painful awareness.

Pessoa raised his hand and made an esoteric sign. I absolve you, Álvaro. Go with the sempiternal gods. If you have loved, even if you have had only one love, you are absolved. Because you are human, it is your humanity that absolves you.

May I smoke? asked Campos.

Pessoa nodded assent. Campos drew from his pocket a silver case and took out a cigarette, inserted it into a long ivory cigarette holder, and lit it. You know, Fernando, he said, I'm nostalgic for the time when I was a decadent poet, when I made that steamship voyage across Oriental seas. Ah, then I could have written poems to the moon, I assure you, in the evening on the bridge, when there were dances on board, when the moon was so spectacular, so much my own. But I was stupid then, I made irony out of life. I didn't know how to enjoy the life that was given me, and so I lost my chance and life fled from me.

And then? asked Pessoa.

Then I began to want to decipher reality, as if reality were decipherable, and I grew depressed. And with depression came nihilism. After that, I believed in nothing anymore, not even in myself.

And now I'm here at your bedside, like a useless old rag. I've packed up for nowhere, and my heart is an empty vessel. Campos went to the night table and crushed out his cigarette in a porcelain saucer. All right, dear Fernando, he said, I needed to say some things to you now that we may be leaving each other. I must go now, the others will also come to see you, I know, not much time remains for you. Farewell.

Campos put his cloak over his shoulders, put his monocle over his right eye, gave a quick wave goodbye, opened the door, lingered a moment, and said once more: Goodbye, Fernando. Then he whispered: Perhaps not all love letters are ridiculous. And he closed the door.

⁓ 3

What time was it? Pessoa didn't know. Was it night? Had the day already come? The nurse came in and gave him another shot. Pessoa no longer felt the pain in his right side. Now he felt a strange peace, as if a fog were descending over him.

The others, he thought, now they would come. Of course, he wanted to say goodbye to all of them before he left. But one encounter made him feel anxious, the one with Master Caeiro, Because Caeiro was coming from the Ribatejo and was in such delicate health. How would he get to Lisbon, perhaps in a carriage? It's true that Caeiro was already dead, but he was also still alive. He would live eternally in the Ribatejo, in that little whitewashed house from which he watched with an implacable eye the passage of the seasons, the winter's rain, and the hot days of midsummer.

He heard knocking at the door and said: Come in.

Alberto Caeiro was wearing a velvet jacket with a fur collar. He was a man from the countryside, as could be seen from his clothing. *Ave*, Master, said Pessoa, *morituri te salutant.*

Caeiro approached the foot of the bed and crossed his arms. My dear Pessoa, he said, I came to tell you something, allow me to make a confession.

Of course, replied Pessoa.

Well then, said Caeiro, when you were awakened during the night by an unknown master who was dictating his poems, speaking to you about the soul, you should know, then, that I was that master. It was I who put myself in contact with you from the Beyond.

I guessed as much, said Pessoa, my beloved Master, I guessed it was you.

But I must beg your pardon for having brought you so much insomnia, said Caeiro, night after night in which you didn't sleep and wrote as if in a trance. I regret having caused you so much trouble, for inhabiting your soul.

You contributed to my work, answered Pessoa, you guided my hand. You brought me insomnia, it's true, but those were fertile nights for me, and my literary work was born in the night. My work is nocturnal work.

Caeiro took off his jacket and hung it on the bedpost. But that's not the only thing I wanted to tell you, he said in a low voice. There's a secret I want to tell you, before the interstellar distances separate us, but I don't know how to tell it.

Tell me in the normal way, said Pessoa, as you'd tell me anything else.

Very well, said Caeiro. I am your father. He paused, smoothed his thin blond hair and continued: I acted in place of your father, your real father Joaquim de Seabra Pessoa, who died of tuberculosis when you were a child. Well then, I took his place.

Pessoa smiled. I knew that, he said. I always considered you my father, even in my dreams you were always my father. You have nothing to reproach yourself for, Master, believe me. You were a father, the one who gave me inner life.

And yet I led a simple existence, replied Caeiro. For a short time I lived in a house in the country in the company of a great aunt. I wrote only about the passage of time, the seasons, the flocks.

Yes, Pessoa agreed, but for me you were an eye and a voice, an eye that describes, a voice that teaches disciples, like Milarepa or Socrates.

I am a man almost without education, said Caeiro. I led a very simple life. You, on the other hand, led an intense life, you interpreted the European avant-garde, invented Sensationism and Intersectionism, you frequented the literary cafés in the capital, while I spent my evenings playing solitaire by the light of an oil lamp. How is it possible that I became your father and your master?

Life is indecipherable, answered Pessoa. Never ask and never believe. Everything is hidden.

Yes, Caeiro resumed, but I insist, how is it possible that I became your father and your master?

Pessoa raised up on his pillows. He was breathing with effort and the room was swimming before his eyes. I will tell you, dear Caeiro, he replied. The fact is that I needed a guide and a coagulant — I don't know if I'm making myself clear — otherwise my life would have shattered into pieces. Thanks to you I found cohesion, it's really I who chose you to be my father and master.

And now I've brought you a gift, said Caeiro, a few verses written in prose, which I'll never publish now that you are leaving me. I'll read them aloud to you. They are the token of my affection for you. Caeiro took a small piece of paper from his pocket, brought it up close to his eyes because he was near-sighted, and he read:

Through these long years, I have always looked at the moon, but with a clear gaze I followed my son and disciple, so that my gaze could be his gaze, so that the hill that defines my horizon might be his horizon, simple and splendid.

It's a very beautiful poem, said Pessoa. I thank you, Master Caeiro, I shall take it with me to the Beyond.

You wrote so many poems under my name, continued Alberto Caeiro. As one who has always admired you, I wanted to say farewell and also to pay homage to you.

Pessoa closed his eyes for a moment. When he opened them again, the room was deserted. He rang the bell to call the nurse. What day is today? he asked.

It's the night of November 28, 1935, replied the nurse. Do you need something?

No, thank you, said Pessoa. I just need to rest.

NOVEMBER 29, 1935

~ 1

Pessoa heard knocking at the door and said: Come in.

The door was half-open, but no one entered. May I come in? asked a tremulous voice.

Please, said Pessoa, come in.

A man appeared at the door and closed it lightly behind him. Pessoa didn't recognize him, and asked: And who are you? Tell me.

I am Ricardo Reis, answered the man, coming into the room. I've returned from my imaginary Brazil.

We haven't seen each other for many years, too many years. Excuse me, but you've changed a lot, I don't recognize you anymore.

Ricardo Reis took a chair by the bed. Excuse me if I sit down, he said, but I made the trip by ferry. I suffer from sea-sickness, I got nauseated and I don't feel very well.

But where have you been hiding? asked Pessoa. In what part of Brazil, so that I couldn't manage to get in touch with you?

Ricardo Reis blew his nose. I have something to confess to you, he whispered. My dear Pessoa, I never went to Brazil. I made everyone believe it, even you. As a matter of fact, I was here in Portugal, hidden in a small village.

Pessoa tried to sit up against the pillows and asked: And where were you?

Ricardo Reis lowered his voice as if someone other than Pessoa might hear him. In Azeitão, he whispered, I was in Azeitão.

Azeitão . . . Azeitão . . . Pessoa answered. The name sounds familiar. I'm reminded of a cheese.

Of course, Ricardo Reis said with pride, Azeitão cheese. Villa Nogueira de Azeitão is a village a few kilometers from Lisbon, just beyond the Tagus, where the Alentejo begins. Ricardo Reis blew his nose again and coughed a little. I was hidden there at a small place owned by friends, I've spent all these years in a farmhouse. In front of the house there's a hundred-year-old mulberry tree, and under that mulberry I wrote all my Pindaric odes and Horatian poems.

And how did you get by? asked Pessoa. Where did you work?

Oh, answered Ricardo Reis, it's easy for a doctor to survive, it's enough just to be a doctor. I was the village doctor, I had patients in the whole Serra da Arrabida.

And did you use your real name? Pessoa asked.

Of course, Ricardo Reis confirmed. I had a sign over the door that said: "Ricardo Reis, MD" and the whole town knew my name.

And yet you were a monarchist . . . said Pessoa. You were against the republic, that's why you said you went into exile in Brazil.

Ricardo Reis smiled a shy and embarrassed smile. It was a hoax, he answered. You know, it was convenient for me, a

Sensist and neoclassical poet, not to love the republic and the vulgarity of republicans. I always wanted a Caesar, a great emperor like Marcus Aurelius who could appreciate my poems. Among the republicans, no one was prepared, they were presumptuous. They'd read only August Comte. How could they appreciate Horace and Pindar?

I understand you, said Pessoa, sighing. There was a long silence. They heard footsteps in the corridor and someone passed by the room, but no one came in to disturb them.

And then? Pessoa asked.

Then, well, answered Ricardo Reis, I wanted to tell you this. I wanted to unveil my secret, you know, I lived the life of a stoic, even if it was in Azeitão.

One can live the life of a stoic anywhere, Pessoa responded.

I weave crowns of flowers, said Ricardo Reis.

What do you mean? Pessoa asked.

This, answered Ricardo Reis: In all my poems I've woven crowns of flowers for Neera and Lydia and now I'm weaving a crown of flowers for your voyage, for when we'll meet again after crossing the icy waters of the Styx.

I accept your ideal crown of flowers, my dear Ricardo Reis, said Pessoa. Please, continue to live in your village and keep on writing your Pindaric odes even without me. I'm happy that you let me in on your secret, but believe me, I always knew it.

Really? said Ricardo Reis, surprised.

Really, answered Pessoa. I never came to see you in Azeitão because I never left Lisbon on principle, because on principle

I never wanted to travel. But I always knew you lived not far away, and a friend who writes sympathetic things about my poetry confirmed it.

Ricardo Reis got up. In that case, I can take my leave now, he said.

I too say farewell, Pessoa replied. Farewell, and I invite you to write your poems even after I am no longer here.

But they will be apocryphal poems, Ricardo Reis replied.

It doesn't matter, said Pessoa, the apocryphal does no harm to poetry, and my work is so vast that it accommodates even apocryphal poems. Farewell, my dear Ricardo Reis, we shall see each other again on the other side of the black river that encircles Avernus.

Pessoa laid his head on the pillow and went to sleep. For an instant or for several hours, he couldn't say.

~ 2

Pessoa awoke, turned on the small bedside lamp and looked for his clock on the night stand. The clock said three, but it had stopped. Pessoa was aware that he'd lost all sense of time. He thought he would ring the bell but gave it up because just then he heard knocking at the door.

May I come in, Senhor Pessoa? asked a voice.

Pessoa said to enter and a man walked in. He was holding a tray in his hands. He paused in the doorway, but Pessoa, without his glasses on and in the shadowy room, didn't recognize him.

And you, who are you? Pessoa inquired.

It's your friend, Bernardo Soares, the man replied. I learned you were in the hospital and I took the liberty of paying you a visit.

Bernardo Soares came up to the bed and placed the tray on the night table. I've brought you dinner, he said. I got it at the restaurant where we always used to meet, I thought maybe you'd want to have dinner like we did in the old days. I took the liberty of choosing the menu.

Actually, I'm not very hungry, Pessoa replied, but to please you I will eat something. What have you brought me?

If you can sit up, I'll set the tray here, Bernardo Soares

replied. They're traditional dishes from our cuisine, simple and delicious.

Pessoa sat up, tied the immaculate napkin that Bernardo Soares had give him around his neck and raised the metal covers that were covering the dishes.

Here's a *caldo verde*, said Bernardo Soares, your favorite soup, I know you like it. And here's tripe Oporto-style. I brought it for you because once you had had it served cold, like a love grown cold, and you wrote about it in a poem, but I wanted you to taste it warm. Look, it's just off the fire and still steaming.

Pessoa smiled. I have a liver disease, he said, and maybe tripe isn't the dish for me, but I'll try a little of it. I still remember when they served it to me cold, but you know, dear Soares, I wasn't myself then. Álvaro de Campos had taken my place.

Pessoa finished his soup and tasted a piece of tripe. It's exquisite, he said, but please, Senhor Soares, you eat it. I'm sure you haven't had lunch today.

Actually, I haven't eaten, replied Bernardo Soares. I couldn't allow myself the luxury of paying for two meals; I bought only yours, so I'll gladly accept.

Bernardo Soares set the tray down before him and ate the tripe with gusto. It makes me nostalgic for our evenings when we dined together at Restaurante Pessoa, he said. I'm sure you chose it because it bore your name. In fact it's a simple restaurant where people like you would never go.

Not exactly true, replied Pessoa, I like simple restaurants. I've always lived a simple life. But, tell me, do you still think about Samarkand?

I've learned a little Uzbek, said Bernardo Soares, just for fun, even if I'll never go to Samarkand, but knowing the language of the region makes me feel closer to the city I've dreamed about my entire life.

And your boss, Senhor Vasques? asked Pessoa.

Oh, replied Bernardo Soares, he's a fine man, he's a man without metaphysics as he would say, but he's a kind person. He even lent me a villa, where I spent a week of vacation.

Where? asked Pessoa.

In Cascais, replied Bernardo Soares, on the road that goes to Guincho.

Cascais, said Pessoa, Cascais, what a lovely place. I spent some time there too, not more than a couple of weeks. It's the first time I've told anybody and I gladly confess it to you who are my friend. My dear Soares, I went to check into the Cascais psychiatric clinic, and there I met António Mora, the pantheist philosopher, and I must say that I spent the serenest days of my life in that town. A black wave had engulfed and overwhelmed me and I had wanted to do nothing but die. Instead I met António Mora and he gave me faith in Nature.

António Mora? asked Bernardo Soares. You've never spoken to me about him, I'd like to learn something about him.

Very well, said Pessoa. António Mora is insane, at least he's officially insane. But he's a lucid madman, he's thought deeply about paganism and Christianity. I'll tell you this, he wears a toga like the ancient Romans did, a white toga down to his feet, ancient-style sandals, and he rarely speaks, though he spoke to me.

And what did he tell you? asked Bernardo Soares.

He told me many things, Pessoa replied. In the first place, he told me that the gods will return, because this story of the single soul and only one god is a transient thing that's going to end with the brief cycles of history. And when the gods return, we'll lose this singleness of the soul, and our souls can be plural again, as Nature desires.

You know, dear Pessoa, said Soares, changing the subject, this past year I've suffered much from insomnia and every morning at dawn I stood by the window to watch the gradations of light over the city. I've described many dawns over Lisbon, and I'm proud of that. It's difficult to write about shades of light but I think I've succeeded. I've made pictures with words.

Like Hopkins? asked Pessoa.

Yes, replied Bernardo Soares, but I got the idea from Keats' diary, and then there's the whole "word-painting" theory of Ruskin, who not by chance was Turner's champion. Yes, I used words as if they were brushes on canvas and Lisbon's dawns and sunsets were my palette.

The sunsets in Cascais are beautiful too, said Pessoa.

That's just what I wanted to talk to you about, Bernardo Soares continued. In Cascais I had an aesthetic experience that I described in my *Book of Disquiet*.

Tell me, said Pessoa.

Well, said Bernardo Soares, the fact is that my employer, Senhor Vasques, had at his disposition a villa by the sea that his firm Vasques & Módica had lent him, and so he was generous enough to let me spend a few days there. He even had his driver take me. I lived alone for a week in a thirty-room villa, oh, it was marvelous.

Tell me the whole story, said Pessoa.

We left on a bright sunny morning, said Bernardo Soares. It was cold, but it was a gorgeous day. I brought Sebastião with me, the parrot that belongs to the coal dealer on the corner. He's a parrot, you know, that can say a few words, even complete sentences, and so I thought he could keep me company. The house has a magnificent terrace that overlooks the ocean. I set Sebastião's perch there, but I unfastened his chain and let him go free. During the day he went out and sat in the trees in the park and at sunset he came back to his perch at the very hour I was out on the terrace making my word pictures. While I was writing, I'd talk with Sebastião and I taught him some of your lines from "The Tobacco Shop": I'm nothing, I'll always be nothing, I can't even wish to be something. He learned them immediately, and so we conversed. I described the sunset over the rocks and the ocean and I said: Go on, Sebastião. And he repeated those lines from "The Tobacco Shop" while I described the tenuous rosy light and violet clouds on the horizon at the fleeting hour of longing.

It's funny, said Pessoa, I wrote for men of the world and only a parrot can recite my poems.

Don't say that, replied Bernardo Soares. There will come a time when all those with noble souls will know your poetry by heart, in all languages. And then, look, Sebastião has a human soul; he's not a parrot, he's an oracle. I'm sure the spirit of a Pythia, foreteller of the future, lives again in him. I feel it.

And then? asked Pessoa.

And then I want to say that they were very beautiful days. It wasn't always easy in the villa because it wasn't heated, and, besides, I had only oil lamps. At night, especially at night, I felt melancholy. But I made friends with a wonderful person, Don Pedro de Cascais, a bachelor and bank director, he's a person who can talk about many subjects. Above all, he loves the Portuguese bullfight, and he even took me to see one. Fearing a bloody spectacle, I refused to go at the beginning, but I had to change my mind. It's not bloody at all, they don't kill the bull, you know, dear Pessoa. The matador makes a symbolic gesture with his arm after he's intoxicated the beast with his dance. At that moment, a herd of cows comes into the arena and the bull joins them and they go out. But you should see the elegance of the horsemen dressed in eighteenth-century costume, the horses' harnesses and the way they prance through their paces around the bull. It was an unforgettable show. But I don't want to tire you.

Tell me more, Pessoa urged.

Well, said Bernardo Soares, one night Senhor Don Pedro invited me to dinner. He came to pick me up in his car. He had a black Chevrolet covered with chrome, just like the one Álvaro de Campos used to drive through the streets of Sintra. It was a windy night and the branches of the trees in the park were creaking. I had on my Sunday best and Senhor Don Pedro was wearing an English blazer. I'm taking you to the best restaurant in Cascais, he said. The terrace surveys the whole village; so you can describe the bay, its lights, the fishing boats. Believe me, dear Pessoa, it was a magnificent restaurant, I've never seen its equal in my entire life. When we arrived, the maitre d' greeted us and offered us real French champagne and oysters. You know, dear Pessoa, I'd never eaten oysters in my life. You, yes, you've had them, you've eaten them at Tavares or at the Brasileira do Chiado. They're exquisite, it seems like one's sipping the sea. I even thought of writing a short piece on taste and aroma, I, who only write about life; and then Senhor Don Pedro said to the maitre d': Bring us *lagosta suada*. But he said it in French, *homard sué*, the way it's made in Peniche. Listen, I'd never tasted shellfish in my life, but Senhor Don Pedro gave me the recipe and I want to give it to you, so that when you're better your sister can cook it for you. You need butter, three onions, tomatoes, and a bit of garlic, oil, white wine, a little aged *aguardente*, which I know you like, two wine glasses of dry port, a dash of hot pepper, black pepper, and nutmeg. First, you steam the lobster, just a little. Then you add the ingredients I gave you and put it in the oven. I don't know why it's called "sweaty," probably because it produces a very tasty broth. Our Peniche fishermen make it this way, and they know how to eat well, and I'd never before tasted such a delicacy. And then Senhor Don Pedro offered me a glass of exquisite port, which we drank on the terrace. Below us were the lights of Cascais bay. Oh, dear Pessoa, it was marvelous. Senhor Don Pedro spoke about his trips to Seville, and I told him about the trip I'd always dreamed of taking to Samarkand. I even offered to lend him my Uzbek language manual. He smiled kindly and said: Samarkand, what a beautiful idea, Senhor Bernardo Soares, but I'll never leave the Iberian peninsula. All I need is the little Spanish I know and a little English for when my London friends come to see me and I take them to play billiards at the Casa do Alentejo in Lisbon. Then the lights on the promenade went out as if by magic. Only a few lights remained on the bay, the lights of the fishing boats, and Senhor Don Pedro said, Senhor Bernardo Soares, I'll take you home now. During the trip back, I told him about the dawns and the sunsets. I felt euphoric, and I thought: I'll write a euphoric chapter in my disphoric diary. Senhor Don Pedro was very discreet and didn't interrupt my chatter. I got out near the park, where the trees were shaking in the wind, and I said: Thank you, Senhor Don Pedro, this has been one of the most beautiful evenings of my life. And he replied: It is I who thank you, dear Bernardo Soares. I'd be honored to be among the first to read your diary, and don't forget that I am a great admirer of Fernando Pessoa. Please do tell him so. He never sees anyone and it's impossible for me to tell him. And so I'm telling you, dear Fernando Pessoa, I bring you Don Pedro's greetings and his admiration.

Thank you, said Fernando Pessoa with a tired smile.

Bernardo Soares straightened the sheets around him. Senhor Pessoa, he said, I'm afraid I've tired you with all my chatter, forgive me, perhaps I've been importunate.

No indeed, Pessoa replied weakly, it was a pleasure to talk to you, but I think I shall receive another visit, a person that I've neglected lately. Thank you, dear Soares, and best wishes for your *Book of Disquiet*.

NOVEMBER 30, 1935

~ 1

The man who came in was an old man of noble bearing, with an enormous white beard and a long Roman toga, also white.

Ave, o sodale, said the old man, I'll take the liberty of infiltrating your dreams.

Pessoa turned on the bedside lamp. He looked at the old man and recognized António Mora. He nodded for him to come near.

Mora raised his hand and said: Phlebus the Phoenecian, a fortnight dead, forgot the cry of the gulls and the deep sea swell to tell me of your fate, O great Fernando. I know the waters of Acheron await you, and then the furious vortex of atoms in which everything disperses and is created anew, and you will perhaps return to the gardens of Lisbon as a flower that blooms in April, or perhaps as rain on the lake and on the lagoons of Portugal. I, walking by, will listen to your voice carried by the wind.

Pessoa rose up a little. The pain in his right side was gone, now he felt only a deep tiredness. And *The Return of the Gods?* he asked.

The book is almost finished, replied António Mora, but I don't know if I can publish it, because no one dares publish the book of a madman.

Listen, said Pessoa, how is it going at the Cascais psychiatric clinic? We saw each other so briefly.

You know, replied António Mora, my diagnosis is paranoia with intermittent psychoneurosis, but luckily there's Dr. Gama, who likes to listen to me. He's a very open-minded person. He, too, believes in the return of the gods, and maintains that madness is a condition invented by men to segregate people who disturb society. I disturb Catholic society, the Church, because I preach the return of the gods. Only you can help me, O great Pessoa, but now you're about to cross the Acheron, and I'll be left alone, in an insane asylum, without anyone who can publish my writings.

Pessoa smiled, rested his head on the pillow and made a reassuring gesture. Dear António Mora, all the writings you gave me on that day we saw each other at the clinic in Cascais I've kept in a trunk. It's a trunk full of people by now, because the characters are struggling to stay inside, but your *Return of the Gods* will not be lost, posterity will rediscover it one day. And seeing that I now possess the gift of divination, I can tell you that a great critic will discover you, an educated and sensitive man named Coelho.

Coelho Pacheco? asked António Mora.

No, a different man, replied Pessoa, very different. A man who doesn't write poetry but does research, a stubborn man who will be able to decipher your handwriting and mine, a man of great courage who will make us known in the world.

In the world? Where in the world? asked António Mora.

In the world, Pessoa answered.

António Mora took a step forward and bowed. And what of you, dear Pessoa, what can you tell me, did you recover at the Cascais psychiatric clinic? I'm surprised I didn't see more of you, did they keep you in isolation?

Pessoa sighed. I didn't stay, he said. I confess, I didn't stay there. I chose to spend some weeks in a house in Rua da Saudade that overlooks the bay, the house of a woman who took care of me. The lady was a widow with two daughters, very kind girls, and she cooked me lunches and dinners I can't even describe to you. Well, why not, I shall describe them to you, dear António Mora. Just think, at lunch I always had a grilled or baked fish with a white wine from Colares, and in the evening, well, dinner was a true banquet. There was always *sopa alentejana* or a *caldo verde*, and then, imagine, baked cod, *pescadinhas de rabo na boca*, and other exquisite delicacies. They'd given me a room that looked out over the bay, an old living room that had been made into a bedroom, with a fireplace and everything. In the evening I'd stay there, on the terrace, looking out at the bays of Cascais and Estoril and listening to dance music or old songs from Coimbra, and I felt happy.

And what was this woman's name? asked António Mora.

It isn't important, replied Pessoa.

I envy you, said António Mora. You've had times of happiness. And, tell me, were you cured?

Well, said Pessoa, at that time a black wave had come crashing over me. I didn't know what to do. Was I crazy? Should I jump in the Tagus? I needed a family, someone to take care of me, to treat me with affection and kindness, and in that family I found a hearth, and then, when I was alone in the house, because sometimes I was alone in the house, there was a dog, a beautiful black dog named Jó, an intelligent mutt to whom I read my esoteric poems. That dog, I'm certain, was the reincarnation of an ancient Egyptian divinity. He brushed his paw against the floor and dictated the verse measure to me, and with that divine and animal-like scansion I'd find the meter of my poems, turning them into music. Then I went to sit on the terrace to watch the bay, the fishing boats returning at dusk, to hear the sailors' voices cheerfully calling to one another, to breathe the odor of tar and fishing nets. It was all beautiful and ancient, and I was cured. I forgot death and began to live again.

I forgot about death too, said António Mora, when I read the fatherly Lucretius, who teaches the return of life in Nature's order, and I understood that all the atoms that compose us, these infinitesimal particles that make up our bodies, will return to the eternal cycle and they will be water, earth, fertile flowers, plants, the light that gives us vision, the rain that bathes us, the wind that stirs us, the white snow that wraps us in its winter mantel. We shall all return here to earth, O great Pessoa, in the numberless forms that Nature desires, and perhaps we will be a dog named Jó, a blade of grass, or the ankles of a young English woman who stares at one of Lisbon's squares, astonished. But please, it's too early for you to leave us. Stay with us a little longer, as Fernando Pessoa.

Pessoa lay his cheek on the pillow and smiled wearily. Dear António Mora, he said, Persephone wants me in her kingdom, and now it's time to go, it's time to leave this theater of images we call our life. You may know the things I've seen with the soul's eyeglasses, the buttresses of Orion high in infinite space, I've walked with these terrestrial feet along the Southern Cross. Like a blazing comet, I've traversed infinite nights, interstellar spaces of the imagination, voluptuousness and fear. I've been a man, a woman, an old person, a little girl, I've been the crowds on the grand boulevards of the capital cities of the West, I've been the serene Buddha of the East, whose calm and wisdom we envy. I've been myself and others, all the others that I could be. I've known honor and dishonor, enthusiasm and exhaustion. I've crossed rivers and impervious mountains, I've watched placid flocks, and I've felt the sun and rain on my head. I've been a female in heat, I've been the cat that plays by the roadside, I've been the sun and the moon, and everything because life is not enough. But now I've had enough, dear António Mora, living my life has been like living a thousand lives. I'm tired, my candle is burnt out. Please, hand me my eyeglasses.

António Mora straightened his toga. Prometheus rose up in him. O divine heaven, he exclaimed, swift-wingèd winds, waters of the rivers, countless smiles of sea waves, earth, universal mother, I invoke you, and the all-seeing circle of the sun, witness what I suffer.

Pessoa sighed. António Mora took his glasses from the night stand and placed them on Pessoa's face. Pessoa opened his eyes wide and his hands fell motionless on the sheet. It was exactly eight-thirty.

CAST OF CHARACTERS

Senhor Manacés
 had a barber shop at the corner of Rua Coelho da Rocha, where Pessoa lived from 1920 to 1935. He was Pessoa's barber for fifteen years.

Carlos Eugénio Moitinho de Almeida
 (Lisbon 1885–1961) was the owner of one of the import-export firms for which Pessoa wrote and translated commercial letters. A good friend of the poet's, he was close to him during the most difficult times in his life.

Coelho Pacheco
 We know nothing about Coelho Pacheco's life. We do know that he wrote only one long poem, "Beyond Another Ocean," dedicated to Alberto Caeiro. It was an obscure and visionary poem, a stream-of-consciousness work that preceded the practice of psychic automatism.

Fernando Pessoa
 Fernando António Nogueria Pessoa was born on June 13, 1888, in Lisbon, to Madalena Pinheiro Nogueira and Joaquim de Seabra Pessoa, a music critic for a city newspaper. When Pessoa was five years old, his father died of tuberculosis. His paternal grandmother, Dionísia, was afflicted with a serious kind of madness and died in an asylum. In 1895 Pessoa moved to Durban, South Africa, because his mother had married the Portuguese Consul there. He did all his studies in English. He returned to Portugal to enroll at the University, but he didn't graduate. He always lived in Lisbon. On March 8, 1914, his first heteronym, Alberto Caeiro, appeared. Ricardo Reis and Álvaro de Campos

followed. The heteronyms were "other selves," voices that spoke in him and that had autonomous lives and biographies. Pessoa invented the entire Portuguese avant-garde. He always lived in modest boarding houses and rented rooms. He had only one love in his life, Ophélia Queiroz, employed as a secretary in the import-export agency where he worked. It was an intense but brief relationship. He published only in magazines during his lifetime. The only volume of work that came out before he died was a chapbook entitled *Message*, an esoteric history of Portugal. He died on November 30, 1935, in the São Luís dos Franceses hospital in Lisbon, of liver disease, probably caused by alcohol abuse.

Álvaro de Campos

Álvaro de Campos was born in Tavira, in the Algarve, on October 15, 1880. He graduated from the University of Glasgow with a degree in Naval Engineering. He lived in Lisbon, but did not practice his profession. He made a trip to the Orient by steamship, which inspired his poem "The Opium Den." He was a decadent, a Futurist, an avant-gardist, a nihilist. In 1928 he wrote the most beautiful poem of the century, "The Tobacco Shop." He had a homosexual relationship, and his entrance into Pessoa's life destroyed his engagement to Ophélia. Tall, with straight black hair parted on the side, he was impeccable and a bit of a snob, and wore a monocle. He was typical of a certain kind of avant-gardist of the age: bourgeois and anti-bourgeois, elegant and provocative, impulsive, neurotic, and anguished. He died in Lisbon on November 30, 1935, the day and year of Pessoa's death.

Alberto Caeiro

Alberto Caeiro da Silva, the master of Fernando Pessoa and all his heteronyms, was born in Lisbon in 1889 and died in the provinces in 1915. He died of tuberculosis like Pessoa's father. He spent his brief life in a village in the Ribatejo, in the house of an elderly great aunt, where he had moved because of his poor health. Not much can be said about the life of this solitary and contemplative man who lived far from the madding crowd. Pessoa describes him as blond, of medium height, with a pale complexion and blue eyes. He wrote poems that seemed elegiac and ingenuous. In reality, Caeiro was an observing eye, a predecessor of the phenomenology that would emerge in Europe a few decades later.

Ricardo Reis

Ricardo Reis was born in Oporto on September 19, 1887, and educated in a Jesuit college. He was a doctor, but we do not know if he practiced medicine for a living. After the establishment of the Portuguese Republic, he withdrew to Brazil, in exile, because of his monarchist ideas. He was a Sensist, materialist, and classical poet. He was influenced by Walter Pater and the remote and abstract classicism that fascinated certain English scientists and naturalists of the fin de siècle.

Bernardo Soares

We know neither the date of his birth nor of his death. He led a very simple life, working as "assistant accountant" in Lisbon, in an import-export textile firm. He dreamed ceaselessly of Samarkand. He is the author of the lyrical and metaphysical diary that he entitled *The Book of Disquiet*. Pessoa met him in a small restaurant called Pessoa and, while dining at its small tables, Bernardo Soares told him about his literary projects and his dreams.

António Mora

The philosopher António Mora ended his days in the Cascais psychiatric clinic, where Pessoa met him. He was the author of *Return of the Gods*, which would have comprised the masterwork of Portuguese neopaganism. Tall, imposing, with a lively expression and a white beard, António Mora recited for Pessoa the beginning of Prometheus's lament from Aeschylus' tragedy. It was in those circumstances, in the clinic, that the old philosopher entrusted Pessoa with his manuscripts.